I0593894

Murder by the River, Mystery One

Detective Paul White is brought out of retirement to solve the deaths of three of his classmates in his sleepy hometown, Helena, Arkansas. Upon his return, he discovers friends he can't trust and a clue left by one of his dead classmates, which helps him solve the case.

Unnecessary Murders in the First Degree, Mystery Two

The town folk in Marvell, Arkansas are upset because seven boys have been found dead. The sheriff thinks a serial killer is on the loose, but he doesn't have any leads. He calls in Detective Paul White to help solve the case. This case will take Detective White across country to find the killer. Will he solve the case before another boy is killed?

A Lover's Revenge, Mystery Three

Detective Paul White is called in to help his former partner with the Chicago Police Department solve the murders of eight women in Houston, Texas who died similarly. The killer thinks he has hidden his tracks well, but not with Detective White on the case. When the case is solved, the killer is not who they expect.

Conviction of an Innocent Man, Mystery Four

Carnell Johnson is serving time in a Georgia prison for a crime he didn't commit and someone is trying to kill him. The mafia and a drug cartel are trying to expand in Atlanta. The FBI is looking to bring the cartel down and has Detective Paul White go undercover to help solve the case. Things get heated in Hotlanta before the case is solved.

CHICAGO'S FINEST

A DETECTIVE PAUL WHITE
ANTHOLOGY

CHICAGO'S FINEST

A DETECTIVE PAUL WHITE
ANTHOLOGY

OTIS JONES

MISSION
POSSIBLE
PRESS

MISSION POSSIBLE PRESS

Creating Legacies through Absolute Good Works

The Mission is Possible.

Sharing love and wisdom for the young and "the young at heart," expanding minds, restoring kindness through good thoughts, feelings, and attitudes is our intent. May you thrive and be good in all you are and all you do...

Be Cause U.R. Absolute Good!

Chicago's Finest, A Detective Paul White Anthology © 2018 by Otis Jones

No part of this book may be reproduced in any written, electronic, recording, or photocopying form without written permission of the publisher. The exception would be in the case of brief quotations embodied in critical articles or reviews and pages where permission is specifically granted by the publisher.

Although every precaution has been taken to verify the accuracy of the information contained herein, the author and publisher assume no responsibility for any errors or omissions. No liability is assumed for damages that may result from the use of information contained within. All rights reserved worldwide.

Books may be purchased in quantity by contacting the publisher directly:

Mission Possible Press, A division of Absolute Good,

PO Box 8039 St. Louis, MO 63156

or by calling 240.644.2500

MissionPossiblePress.com

ISBN: 978-0-9996766-2-2

First Edition

Printed in the United States

DEDICATION

I dedicate this book to my fun-loving sisters Georgia Jones and the late Cherie Green. I'm honored to be your brother.

ACKNOWLEDGMENTS

To my inspiration, Jordan Jones. Son, you are a great man and I am so proud of you. To Napoleon White, the big brother type of human being who was so helpful, down to his last dime, throughout my whole life, thank you.

Pastor Johnson at the Circle of Life Church of St. Louis, Missouri, who teaches that you can achieve anything through God. You're a good listener, you give good advice and you always tell the truth whether a person likes it or not. Thank you.

To Sister Buchanan who read my first draft and inspired and encouraged me to keep writing, I appreciate you.

To Jennifer Thomas of Mission Possible Press for your work in helping me to develop my story lines. You are a gem.

Thanks to my publisher, Jo Lena Johnson for helping me to become a published author, something I wasn't sure I could do.

CONTENTS

MURDER

BY THE RIVER

A DETECTIVE PAUL WHITE
MYSTERY #1

CHAPTER ONE

Paul White, a retired homicide detective living in Niagara Falls, New York, is looking out the windows of his luxury loft located on the beautiful Niagara River. He is enjoying his new life after working on the Chicago Police Force for 36 years. Proud of himself and his accomplishments, grateful for that big stock investment tip that allowed him to double his pension and continue earning, he breathes a sigh of relief and gratitude. Looking out at the river, he is thinking about the hard time he had growing up in the cotton fields of Helena, Arkansas, a small town along the southern part of the Mississippi River in the eastern part of the state. The thought of his childhood, the memories of hard times, joy and pain he and his family endured, makes him melancholy. As he sips his second cup of coffee, he realizes it has been a long time since he has been home—twelve years, to be exact. In the middle of that thought, the phone rings.

"Good morning, who's calling?"

"Hey, Paul, it's Al Jennings."

"What's up, Al? How have you been doing? It's been a long time."

"Paul, I'm calling to tell you about the deaths of three of our classmates: John Salon, Joe Wilson and Jerry Jones. They were found dead yesterday in different parts of town here in Helena. Each one was shot in the back of head, and each body had the initials C. B. carved in their chests. Paul, you know murders like this just don't happen here. Something is going on."

"I can't believe it," Paul says. "Al, have there been any arrests? What have the police been saying about the murders?"

"The police aren't saying anything, and there were no witnesses. Damn it, Paul, I'm torn up about this. We knew these guys all our lives. They went to church on Sunday, took care of their families and were good men. Our classmates were pillars of the community. John was an excellent educator and the high school principal. Joe was a chemist at Arkansas Power and Light. Jerry was a professor at the local community college."

"You know, Al, I've been thinking about coming home anyway. I guess now is the time. I'll book a flight into Memphis and be there in three days."

"Okay, do you want me to pick you up?"

"No, thanks. I'll rent a car and drive to Helena. Don't tell anybody I'm coming home. If the authorities aren't saying anything or releasing anything to the press, there may be more to this than the murders."

"I'm glad you're coming; we really need you."

"Al, thanks for calling, and you take care. I'll see you in a few days."

As Paul hangs up the phone, he ponders his classmates' demise. *Why were they murdered? Shot in the back of the head? What the hell is going on? I've got to get to the bottom of this.*

Paul books his flight to Memphis and begins to pack.

CHAPTER TWO

When Paul arrives in Memphis, he calls Al Jennings right away. "Good morning, Al. I just arrived in Memphis, and I'm getting my rental car. I should be in Helena in about two and a half hours. When I get there, I'm going to stop by the police department to talk with the detective in charge of the murder investigations."

"Okay, Paul. See you soon."

When Paul arrives at the Helena Police Department, he walks into the lobby and approaches the desk sergeant, Mike Hamilton, his cousin twice removed by marriage. Hamilton knew what was happening and was glad to hear from Paul when he called the day before. Mike knew Paul, being an outsider, would be able to deal with the corruption and cover-up.

Acting as if he does not know Mike, Paul says, "Good morning, Sergeant. I'm Detective White, and I would like to talk with the detective in charge of the investigation of the three recent murders."

The desk sergeant quickly responded, "That would

be Detective Carl Woodson. You can wait for him in the conference room while I see if he's available. Let me show you the way."

Paul and Mike walk to the conference room. Before he leaves, Mike sets a file in front of Paul. "You'll find everything you need in here. I'll give you a few minutes before calling Detective Woodson."

"Thanks, Mike. I really appreciate your help. Tell Sharon I said hello."

"I sure will. Let me know if you need anything else."

About 15 minutes later, Sergeant Hamilton pops his head into Detective Woodson's office. "Good morning, Detective Woodson. A Detective White is here to see you about the recent murders."

Woodson barks out, "Tell him that I'll be out in a minute."

"He's in the conference room waiting."

As Sergeant Hamilton leaves, Detective Woodson begins shuffling papers around, mumbling, "Detective White? Hmm." He gets up from his desk and rushes out the door to see Paul.

"Good morning, Detective White, I was told that you were waiting to see me."

"Yes, I am. I have some questions concerning the recent murders that have taken place here. I've known John, Joe and Jerry all my life. So it was a shock to me when I heard they had been murdered."

Detective Woodson smiles, recognizing Paul, and says, "Paul, I thought you retired from the Chicago PD. You know you have no legal jurisdiction here, and we don't need any help from you."

Detective White looks up and states, "That is true. I am retired, and I have no jurisdiction here. I'll just talk to the state's attorney general or the governor about putting me on the case if you aren't going to cooperate."

"Do whatever you want, Paul. Call your friends, but you won't get any cooperation from me or my department. You are retired; please stay that way."

Paul gets up to leave and says, "You wouldn't have something to hide, would you, Carl? Have a nice day."

He knows for sure now that there is something funny about these murders. Too many questions, and from what he can tell, there is evidence missing from the files. He'll have to take a closer look once he gets to his hotel. He gives Al Jennings a call on his way.

"Hello, Al, I just spoke with Detective Woodson. He practically told me to get lost. I'm on my way to the state's attorney general to ask if he can assign me to the investigation."

Al laughs and says, "I don't think that you have to go that far. Do you remember Jordan Madison, one of our classmates?"

"Jordan and I go back to the third grade, and we were in law school together. We both had a hard time."

"Well, he's the Phillips County district attorney. I'm quite sure he would want your help. I happen to have his number right here."

"I didn't know Jordan was back here. Let me have his number so I can give him a call now. I hope he can see me right way."

After getting the number, Paul says, "Thanks. I'll talk to you later, Al."

Once in the Phillips County District Office, Paul greets the DA's secretary, Cathy. "Good morning. I'm Paul White, a former classmate of Jordan's. I called a few minutes ago to see if he was in the office."

"Let me see if he's available. Please have a seat." The secretary buzzes the DA. "Good morning. Paul White is here to see you. He says y'all are former classmates."

"Please send him in, Cathy."

As she hangs up, she tells Paul he can go in and see the district attorney.

"Paul, long time no see," Jordan says as he comes from around his desk to shake Paul's hand. "I guess you've heard about the murders."

"Yes, I have."

"I can't really go into all the details of the murders since it's an open investigation."

"I know, but we grew up with these men. If we work together, we can solve these murders and bring some closure to their families. They didn't deserve this."

"You may have a point, Paul. Let me see if I can add you to the investigation as a consultant."

"How soon can you let me know, Jordan? I'm staying at the Best Western in town."

"Okay, Paul, I'll give you a call as soon as I get things checked out."

"Alright, Jordan, I'll wait to hear from you."

After Detective White leaves District Attorney Madison's office, another local government official comes out of the adjoining office and says, "I know you're not going to allow Detective White be a part of the murder investigation."

"Yes, I am because he is great investigator; he has skills that you can't imagine. But, this way, we can keep an eye on him and make sure he doesn't get too close to the truth."

"You better make sure that he doesn't get too close, because if he does, someone might be investigating *his* murder."

CHAPTER THREE

When Detective White arrives at his hotel room, he takes out the case files he received from Mike Hamilton at the police station. He had taken pictures of everything while he was waiting for Detective Woodson to join him in the conference room. On his way back from the DA's office, he stopped to make copies. As he begins to read the files, he notices that there was no record of blood, hair, fibers, fingerprints, or witnesses, and no interviews had been conducted. There wasn't even a description of the murder weapon that might have been used, and there weren't any suspects. *Who would destroy important evidence in an important case like this?* His experience was telling him it was someone close to the case since forensic evidence was missing or destroyed.

Taking a closer look at the evidence, he comes across an actual piece of evidence. There are pictures of a gold watch with strange markings on the front and back. According to the investigator's notes, the gold watch didn't belong to any of the murder victims. *Is there a conspiracy? Who did it? And why?* He takes a closer look at the pictures, but he cannot make out the markings on the watch. Finding the watch could be the key, but who could he trust? Mike told him he thought there was something big going on, and when he was in Jordan's office, he got the feeling it wasn't just the two of them. *Was Jordan a part of this?*

He needed to talk to someone not associated with the investigation. Thinking about his friend who is an FBI agent, David Woody, he decides to give him a call.

"David, Paul White. Do you have moment?"

"It's been a long time, Paul. How have you been doing? I heard that you retired."

"I'm doing good. I'm living in Niagara Falls, New York, now."

"Wow, I remember you saying you wanted to retire there. I can't wait to retire."

"Yeah, most days it's a great feeling. However, today isn't one of those days. I was calling because a buddy of mine from my hometown called me about the murder of three of our classmates. I can't trust anyone down here to help, so that's why I am reaching out to you. I need your help."

"Sure, I'll do what I can."

"I have copies of the files for each victim, but there is nothing of substance in the files. No fingerprints, blood, clothes fibers, nothing."

David exclaims, "That's almost impossible! A murderer in a small town would most certainly leave a trail of evidence. From what you're telling me, it seems there is someone there who knows how to cover up a crime scene."

"I'm beginning to think these murders will never be solved unless I take action. I do have a picture of a gold watch with strange markings that was found at one of the murder scenes. If I can find that gold watch and who it belonged to, it could be helpful in solving these murders."

"In a couple of days, I'm going to be in Little Rock on official government business. I could stop in Helena and help you."

"That sounds great, David. Maybe we'll find that damn watch. See you in a couple of days."

Detective White sits back in his hotel room chair, pondering who else he could get to help him in Helena. It was clear that no one in power at the district attorney's office or the police department could be trusted. He reexamined the pictures of the gold watch, knowing it was the key. Needing to clear his head, he decides to drive to Tunica to relax and figure out what to do next.

CHAPTER FOUR

Upon arriving at the most popular casino in Tunica, Detective White thinks he sees an old friend in the parking lot. *Is that Dr. Johnson?* He and Mary worked together in Chicago solving countless murders. Dr. Johnson is one of the leading pathologists in the country. She was a pro at solving murder cases with minimum amounts of forensic evidence. *What in the world is she doing here in Tunica, of all places?*

Getting closer, he realizes it is Mary Johnson and greets her. "Hey, Mary! How's it going? What are you doing here?"

Dr. Johnson smiles warmly and says, "I came to Memphis for a pathology conference, and I thought that I would take a little time for myself and have fun at the casino."

Paul grins.

She continues, "I hope to get a bit of rest, maybe a massage, and see how good my luck is at the poker table. Right now, I'm starving, so I'm on my way to the lunch buffet. Would you like to join me?"

"Sure." Delighted about the coincidence, Paul chuckles to

himself, thinking about her and old times.

"Great minds think alike. I was coming to press my luck at the casino as well."

"I heard you retired and moved to New York."

"Yes, I did."

"Aren't you from somewhere around here?"

"Yes, that's the reason I'm in the area. I received a call from a good buddy telling me three of our childhood friends were murdered."

"I'm so sorry to hear that."

"Thank you. I'm actually looking into their murders. The files are missing evidence, and it appears the crime scene was wiped clean. And you know, there is no such thing as a perfect crime."

Dr. Johnson turns to Paul. "It seems that there is more to these murders than meets the eye. You know I love a challenge. How about I help you for old time's sake? I can get some time off from work and assist you with your investigation."

"We did work well together, Mary."

They both laugh. As they walk through the casino lobby, Paul fills her in about his visit to the police station and the DA's office. He told her he felt uneasy about his conversation with the DA. Something was off about his demeanor. Mary knew Paul well enough to know that he would not stop until the case was solved.

He tells her, "Unbeknownst to the DA, also an old friend, I had gotten special permission from the state's attorney general to be a consultant on the murder investigations. We go way back as well. However, because of the seriousness of the case and the way the local leaders were keeping things so close to the vest, we didn't give anyone in town a heads-up about my involvement. I wanted to tread gently and see if they would open up. When they didn't, my suspicions, seconded by a relative in the police department, seemed to be confirmed. I believe an insider is calling the shots of a cover-up."

"Who don't you know, Paul?"

They walk into the restaurant and head toward the buffet. They chat about the old days and catch up on their recent activities, enjoying the light conversation throughout lunch. Afterward, Dr. Johnson makes a few calls to clear her schedule. After hanging up from her last call, she asks, "Where do you want to start?"

"Let's start with the murder of John Salon. We need to talk to his family and closest friends to see if they know who would want to kill him and why. Let me call my friend Al."

"Al, this is Paul."

"Hey, Al."

"Can we get together tomorrow? I want to start my investigation with John Salon's murder."

"Okay. What time is good for you?"

"I'm in Tunica now. I came up here to clear my mind and ran into an old friend from Chicago who has agreed to help us with the investigation. We'll pick you up around eight tomorrow morning."

"Who's your friend?"

"A pathologist I worked with when I was a cop."

"Okay, Paul. See you tomorrow morning."

"Mary, how about we hit the casino?"

"Sure."

After a couple of hours in the casino, Paul and Mary decide to part ways until the next day.

"Mary, I'm going to head back to my hotel in Helena. I'll be back to pick you up about 7:15 in the morning."

"You can stay if it's too far for you to drive."

"It's not that far. Thanks, though. Let me walk you to your room."

* * * *

Both Paul and Al were unaware that Al Jennings' phone was being tapped. The person listening knew he had to report what he had overhead to the man he called Boss. He was not eager to deliver the news, but he knew that he had to get the job done quickly.

"Boss, we've been listening to the conversation between Al Jennings and that Detective White. They are meeting tomorrow, and a pathologist from Chicago has agreed to help the detective with the case. They're going over to John Salon's first thing in the morning. What do you want us to do?"

"Follow them, and don't let them out of your sight. I want to know if they find anything, and I want to know immediately."

"Okay. We'll keep you updated."

"Stay with them like white on rice. I want to know their every move."

"Okay, Boss."

He turns to his partner. "Boss wants us to keep a tail on Detective White and Al Jennings. Doesn't your mother live across the street from the Salons?"

"Yes," his partner says. "She's out of town for a few days on a trip to Hot Springs."

"Great. We can keep an eye on them from her house. Let's get out of here, and I'll see you in the morning."

CHAPTER FIVE

When Paul pulls up to the front of the casino hotel, he notices Mary is prepared. "I see you have your kit."

"Paul, you know I never go anywhere without it. I never know when I might need it."

They head back to Helena in anticipation of what the day will bring.

Detective White, still unaware Al's phone is tapped, calls him. "Good morning, Al. I'm parked outside. Come on out so we can get going."

Looking out from his window, Al says, "I'll be out in a minute. And, Paul, you didn't tell me the pathologist was a beautiful, young lady."

Paul chuckles. "I'll introduce you when you get to the car."

Al locks up the house and heads to the car.

As he gets in the back, Paul says, "Al, this is Dr. Mary Johnson. We solved a lot of cases in Chicago, and she's an expert in forensic evidence. Mary, this is Al, one of my oldest friends and the person who called me about this case."

Mary turns in her seat to shake Al's hand. "Good morning, Al."

"Hello, pretty lady. It's a pleasure to meet you," Al says with a wide smile as he shakes her hand.

"You too. I was at a conference in Memphis, and since I've given my presentation, I decided to help Paul out. Plus, I can't pass up a challenge, and there are a lot of holes in these cases."

"That's why I called Paul. Something isn't adding up, and I'm glad you're going to help."

* * * *

They arrive at John Salon's house and exit Paul's car. As Paul closes his door, he has a feeling someone is watching. After looking around, he shakes off the feeling. Just as he's walking to the house, his cell phone rings.

"Hello."

"Paul, this is Jordan. I was calling to let you know you can be a consultant in the investigation."

"Thank you, Jordan."

"No problem. Let's get together in a couple of days so I can bring you up to speed."

"Okay. I will look for your call," Paul says; as he hangs up, he steps onto the front porch.

"Hey guys, that was DA Madison, and he has given me his approval to be a consultant in the investigation. I'm supposed to get together with him in a couple of days, but that should give us time to make some headway ourselves. I know there's more to this than he's saying, especially since he didn't tell me to come over this afternoon."

Al responds, "Great!" Mary says nothing. Al pulls out the key John's wife had given him a few days ago, and they enter the house. John's family wasn't ready to come back to the house where he was murdered and were staying at a relative's in town.

Across the street, one of the henchmen dial the Boss. "Sir, they just arrived. White and Jennings have a woman with them."

"Does she look familiar to you?"

"No."

"Well, watch them closely and report back to me."

"I will." He hangs up the phone, picks up his high-powered binoculars and whispers to himself as the trio enter the house, "I've got you all in my sights."

Detective White and his crew begin to take a careful look around, each of them hoping there was something that had been overlooked, something that would turn the odds in their favor.

They search the house with a fine-tooth comb, looking for any shred of evidence. There had to be something there. Though no one spoke as they worked, it was clear each of them hoped to find a hair, a fingernail, a drop of blood, any clue that would lead them in the right direction.

Detective White finally breaks the silence. "Al, where did they find John's body?"

Al walks toward the family room in the back of the house. "Paul, the body was discovered behind that bar over there in the corner by the window."

After approaching the bar, Detective White peers behind it. As he begins to walk around, he steps on a floor board that is loose. "Hey Al, Mary, there are a couple of loose floorboards back here. I need some help moving these things off them. Maybe there's something in there."

Al comes over to help. "You never know what you'll find under a floorboard. People hide money, guns, jewelry, you name it, under the floor."

Once Paul and Al have moved everything out of the way, Paul begins to remove floorboards. He finds a cardboard box with what seems to be bloodstains on it hidden in the floor. The box is very heavy, and there is a short metal object beneath it.

Paul says, "Looks like blood. What do you think, Mary?"

"Let me get the luminol from my kit."

Al looks at Mary and asks, "What's luminol?"

"It's used to detect blood. It reacts to the iron in blood. I never leave home without it." She walks over to the box and sprays some on the stains, which begin to glow.

"Wow! That's just like it happens on TV," Al exclaims.

She then opens the box, and the first thing she sees is a letter addressed to Detective White. She turns to him and says, "Paul, there is a letter in here addressed to you."

"For me?" Detective White takes the letter from Mary, thinking if the handwriting is John's. *Are you talking to me from the grave, John?* He reads the letter:

Dear Paul, I am writing to you because you are the only person I can trust. I know it's been a long time since we talked, but I am afraid for my life. Me, along with some of our classmates, have discovered that Helena has become a major distribution center for the drug cartel. We have also discovered that the cartel is also in the business of kidnapping and enslaving young teenage girls for prostitution. Girls have been kidnapped from various parts of the county and sold to the highest bidder. The drug cartel has influence inside the local government. We were made aware of all this when Joe Wilson's daughter was found dead. Someone dropped her body in Long Lake River. Joe told us the coroner's report said that she had overdosed on heroin along with several other drugs.

As we began to ask questions about her death, we got harassed by local law officials. I am writing this letter because we fear for our lives. If something happens to any one of us, I want you to know that I have placed some things in a trunk. The trunk is in a hole under my mom's old house on Pillow Hill.

After putting the letter down, Detective White continues to look through the contents of the box. He freezes when he sees the gold watch. *Is this the same gold watch from the photo?* He shakes his head in amazement and exclaims, "Hell, no! I can't believe it's the gold watch. Hey Mary and Al, I found the gold watch, but I still can't figure out what the markings on the back symbolize."

Dr. Johnson reaches for the watch. "Let me see it, Paul. Maybe I can figure what the markings represent." He hands her the watch and continues digging through the box.

He discovers a large manila envelope. When he opens the envelope, he discovers a number of pictures of naked girls and several CDs. The metal object beneath the box is a .357 Magnum. *Is this the weapon?*

Detective White grows anxious, insisting that they leave the house immediately. That feeling of being watched has come over him again. "I've got to get a better look at these things, but not here. I don't want to be seen carrying this box out because of the blood on it. Al, can you find me a bag or something that I can use to carry these items?"

"Sure, let me look."

"I'm going to need more time to figure out these markings on the watch," Mary says.

"We can look at everything once we get back to your hotel." Al comes back with a bag, and Paul puts everything in it. They replace the floorboards and move everything back in place before leaving the house.

* * * *

The individual spying on the trio calls in his report. "Boss, they're leaving the house, and Detective White has a bag with him."

The Boss is angered by this. He yells, "Follow them and find out what is in that bag! Whatever is in there could cause big problems for the organization."

"We're following them now. I'll keep you posted."

"You better. If we go down, you all go down too."

CHAPTER SIX

As he is driving toward Mrs. Salon's house, Paul notices that the same car has been following them for miles, since they left John's house. *Someone is watching us.* Deciding to change plans, he tells Al and Mary, "We're being followed, so we aren't going to John's mother's house now. I need to lose this tail."

Al turns around to look out the back window. Paul begins driving a little faster, but not too fast because he knows the cops are always looking to give out tickets. He decides to head out of town to try to lose them on the highway. After driving several miles, Paul looks in his rearview mirror and doesn't see the car behind him. "I think I've lost them."

"Thank goodness," Mary exclaimed. "You were weaving in and out of traffic so much, I felt like we were in a mid-speed Chicago car chase!"

"Sorry about that. I want to switch cars and park this one at the casino. Can we use your car, Mary, to take Al back home?"

"Of course, I don't mind at all."

A little while later, they arrive at the casino hotel and park in the vicinity of Mary's car. They all get in and head back to Helena to drop Al off at home. As Al enters his house, he's unaware that a man is watching him from across the street. The henchman calls the Boss and says, "Al Jennings just got home."

"Keep an eye one him! You and your friend are going to be the death of me. How did y'all get on the police force?" He shakes his head in frustration. "Don't mess up this time. You should probably pay him a visit and see what you can find out. I'm putting someone else on White."

"Okay, Boss." He purposely failed to tell the Boss that they switched cars. *That will fix him.* He gets out of his car and makes his way toward Al's house, getting in easily through an unlocked window.

* * * *

Al is in the shower when he hears a noise. He exits the shower, wrapping a towel around himself, and leaves the bathroom to investigate. When he gets to his living room, he is greeted by the henchman. Startled, Al yells. "Who the hell are you, and what in hell are doing in my damn house?"

The man quickly pulls a gun from his jacket and fires three shots at Al. Al falls to the floor. The henchman leaves the way he came. He knows the Boss will be upset that he killed him without getting any information. *I'll tell him it was self-defense.*

* * * *

Paul and Mary arrive back at the casino hotel. As they are walking through the lobby, Paul notices that they are being followed by a man. "I think we're being followed by the guy in uniform behind us."

Mary spies a look over her right shoulder and then steps closer to Paul and says, "Jesus, he really looks creepy. I wonder why he's following us."

Paul whispers, "I don't know. Maybe we can lose him in this crowd and get to the stairs to go to your room."

"Paul, my room is on the twelfth floor."

"I know. We'll just go up a few flights and then get on the elevator."

They are able to lose the man in the crowd, get to the stairs and go up a couple of flights before going through a door to take the elevator to Mary's floor.

When the two enter the room, they waste no time reexamining all the items they recovered from the cardboard box at John Salon's home. After a few minutes, Detective White tells Mary, "I'm going back into the hallway to make sure we weren't followed."

Mary looks up from the evidence. "Paul, please be careful; that man could be out there. Please hurry up and come back."

Detective White searches the hallway carefully. Not seeing anyone, he returns to Mary's room.

While Paul looks at the photos, Mary focuses on the watch. Somehow the back of the watch opens. Excited, Mary yells, "You are not going to believe this! The initials C. B. are inside the watch. Didn't you tell me that each murder victim was found with the initials C. B. carved on their chests?"

Paul puts the photos down and turns to Mary. "That's right. I knew that damn watch was going to be one of the keys in solving these murders. Great work, Mary. Now let's take a look at these DVDs."

Shortly into one of the videos, Detective White recognizes the man in the video, who is having sex with three young girls. He jumps to his feet suddenly and tells Mary, "That's Jordan, the DA!"

"What?!"

"We're going to need major help with this case now because the local officials are in knee deep and, unfortunately, on the wrong side of the law. I need to call Al. It's going to be much more difficult to solve now. I'm supposed to meet with Jordan in a couple of days. Hopefully, I'll come up with a plan before our meeting."

"You'll come up with something, I'm sure."

"I'm going to head back to my hotel, but I'll return in the morning so we can come up with a plan. I'll take all of this with me."

"Okay, Paul, I'll see you in the morning. I'll order room service and have breakfast delivered here so we can work while we eat."

"Sounds great, Mary. You know what I like to eat."

"Scrambled eggs, sausage and bacon, hash browns, toast, coffee and orange juice; see you in the morning."

Paul leaves her room and heads toward his car. Meanwhile, in a hallway deep in the casino hotel, the uniformed man who had been following Paul and Mary is talking on the phone. "Hey Boss, I've been looking all over the hotel for them; I think I lost them."

"You people are useless! Stay there and keep looking. They have to be there. I have a plan to get rid of Detective White because he is getting too close for comfort, but I need to know where he is."

"Okay, Boss. I'll keep looking."

CHAPTER SEVEN

Early the next morning, while Mary opens the door for room service, Paul calls FBI agent Woody. "Good morning, David, this is Detective White. I'm calling about the murders again. I'm in Tunica with Dr. Mary Johnson, a pathologist I worked with in Chicago. She's been helping me investigate, along with my friend Al. We have discovered some incriminating evidence that involves some local officials, and I need your help."

"Paul, I'm in Little Rock now, but I have meetings all day. I'll be back in Memphis late tonight. Meet me in Memphis in the morning but come by yourself. There are some things I want to share with you."

Paul is perplexed by his friend's request, but the way this case is unfolding, nothing could surprise him.

"Paul, don't tell anyone where you're going and make sure you aren't followed."

"Okay. I'll be there."

"Paul, breakfast is all set."

"Be right there." He checks his phone for a message from

Al, but there are no texts or missed calls.

As he sits down for breakfast with Mary, he says, "I've been trying to reach Al since last night, but I haven't heard from him. It doesn't make sense. Now I really need to get in touch with Al. I want him to come here and stay with you because I have to go to Memphis. He's not answering, and it scares me."

A bit worried herself, Mary asks, "Why are you going to Memphis?"

"When I flew in, my garment bag didn't make it, and I just received a call that it's been found. I need to go get it."

"They won't deliver it to you?"

"No, it's too far."

"I didn't get a good night's sleep thinking about that man we saw yesterday. I don't want to be here by myself."

"That's why I was trying to get in touch with Al."

"Can I go with you?"

"I'll stay tonight so you won't be alone, but you should be okay during the day while I'm gone. It'll only be a few hours, and I'll be back before evening."

"Okay." They spend the day looking at more of the evidence. After a late dinner in the room, they prepare for bed. Paul gets covers from the closet for the sleeper sofa in the living room when Mary says, "Paul, you don't have to sleep on the sofa. I have a king-sized bed. There's room for both of us with room left over."

"I could use a good night's sleep. Okay, you've convinced me."

* * * *

The Boss has called the members of the cartel into a meeting. He looks into the eyes of each of the twelve members of the cartel sitting at the long oval table. "Gentlemen, thank you all for coming on such short notice. We have some serious problems to discuss concerning this Detective White. He is getting too close." He begins to spell out the details of his plan and asks everyone to use caution and discretion when handling cartel business. He then goes on to reassure the council by saying, "I have a great deal of resources to get rid of Detective White. He could cause our organization to crumble, and I will not stand for that. Each of us has a lot invested in this organization, and thus far, the business has been running seamlessly."

One of the key members to the cartel says, "I don't think that we have anything to worry about. It seems you have everything covered, and you have the backing of everyone here to get rid of that damn detective. One man will not bring this organization down."

"If there's no more business, I recommend that we end this meeting. I'll keep you updated."

The members leave the room of their secret location feeling confident about their future endeavors with no concern about Detective White and his investigation.

* * * *

Back at the hotel, Paul and Mary are now lying in the bed together with their backs to each other. Mary says to Paul, "You know, it's been a long time since I've slept with any man. My job consumes my life, and I hardly time for myself, let alone a relationship."

Paul nods his head, responding, "I know what you're saying. My life was exactly like that too. And even now that I'm retired, I haven't dated much."

"Paul, if you don't mind, could you lie a little closer? I'm a little afraid." He rolls over and moves a little closer to Mary. "Do you mind holding me so I won't feel scared?"

Paul slides his body flush against Mary and puts his arm around her. "Better?"

"Yes."

To his surprise, she rolls over and begins kissing him. She kisses him deeply on the lips. Before long, the two are making passionate love. For a little while, they forget about the case. Two old friends reconnect like never before, neither worrying if it will happen again.

When they awake the next morning, they smile at each other, shower and prepare for the long day ahead.

CHAPTER EIGHT

Paul tries calling Al Jennings several more times on his way to Memphis. *Why isn't he answering my calls?* He arrives at the local FBI office to meet with Agent Woody with a look of concern on his face. It is unlike Al not to return his call. He greets the receptionist, "Good morning, young lady. I'm Detective Paul White from Chicago. I have an appointment with Agent David Woody."

The receptionist had been expecting him. "Yes sir, they're waiting on you. Please go right in through the double doors."

When Detective White enters the room, he sees there are two other men with Agent Woody.

"Good morning, Detective. Please come in and take a seat. I would like to introduce you to Agents George Power and Victor Mayberry." The men greet one another. "They'll be joining us for this meeting. We've been watching the activities of the Arkansas drug cartel for some time. There are Helena police officers and government officials on their payroll. We know most of the key players, but we don't know who is running the cartel. We have everything in place to take down the cartel, but in order do that, we need to take out its leadership. Paul, I know you have been doing your own investigation. What have you found?"

Detective White sits, processing what he has heard, and lets out a sigh. *No wonder he wanted me to come alone.* He takes the contents from the box found in the floorboard out of the bag. "Gentlemen, I have been working with two close friends, Al Jennings and Dr. Mary Johnson, a pathologist from Chicago with whom I've worked with to solve many cases."

Paul didn't notice the look the agents gave one another at the mention of the people helping him with the case as he continues talking. "On the DVDs is footage of young girls having sex with various men. We have identified one of them as the Helena district attorney, Jordan Madison." He then takes out the watch and explains the initials in the watch, C. B., were also carved into all three victims' bodies.

Agent Woody smiles and tells the other agents, "This might be all the evidence we might need to bring down the cartel." He focuses on Paul. "Until now, Detective White, the cartel has been one step ahead of us in our investigation. The DEA has been looking at this crime syndicate for years without one indictment."

Agent Woody reveals to Detective White that the initials C. B. belong to a municipal judge that they have been watching. He is a person of wealth and political power. His family holds most of the land in the Delta and has since before the Civil War.

"Paul, I believe that you are familiar with the Phillips County municipal judge, Carrington Beasley. With this evidence you've provided, we are sure he is the head of the cartel."

"Gentlemen," says Detective White, "I'm happy that I am able to assist with this investigation. I hadn't expected that

I would unearth a major crime syndicate. I will leave these items with you, but I need to return to Helena. One of the victims, John Salon, wrote a letter to me that I found in the same box as these items. He said there was more evidence in a trunk buried at his mother's house. I'm going to head over there, but I need to stop by my friend Al's house first. He hasn't been returning my calls."

Paul begins to get up but sits down when he notices the looks the agents are giving one another. "What's going on?"

Agent Woody couldn't let Paul return to Helena alone; he had more news to share with him. "Paul, I'm going to send two agents back with you. It's not safe for you to keep snooping around unprotected. Yesterday, one of my agents found the body of your friend Al Jennings; he had been shot three times."

Detective White jumps to his feet in outrage. "What in the hell are you saying? Please tell me that my lifelong best friend has not been murdered!" Detective White was almost in tears. Putting his hand on Paul's shoulder, Agent Woody says, "I'm so sorry that we had to tell you the bad news. Paul, it is imperative that when you return to Helena that you do not discuss anything with anyone; no one must know about our meeting. The cartel has eyes and ears everywhere."

"Mary has been helping me with the case. What do I tell her?"

"You're smart; you'll come up with something." Agent Woody uses the phone in the room to make a call. When he hangs up, he says, "Paul, the agents who are going back with you will be in shortly. They'll follow you in their car. They will have eyes on you at all times."

The door opens, and two agents come into the room. "Paul, meet Agents Fred Williams and Derrick Johnson. Fellas, this is Detective Paul White, who we spoke about earlier."

After exchanging pleasantries, they leave the room. Paul and his bodyguards head to their cars, and the other agents go into Agent Woody's office. Agent Mayberry says, "He doesn't realize how much danger he's in, does he?"

Agent Woody replies, "No, he doesn't, but he'll find out soon." Agents Mayberry and Power look at each other.

As Detective White drives back to Tunica, the agents tailing him, his mind is overwhelmed by the information he just received. Shaking his head, he can't believe Al is dead. *Maybe whoever was following us yesterday killed him. I've got to call Jordan and delay that meeting today.* He calls him, but he's not in the office, so he leaves a message with his secretary that something came up in Memphis that he had to tend to and he wouldn't be able to make the meeting with Mr. Madison today. Promising to call to reschedule, Paul hangs up.

Who would have thought the cartel would be in Helena of all places? I know that Agent Woody advised me to remain silent about this case, but there are three retired police officers back in Chicago I know who can be trusted, and they are far enough away that they could not possibly have any connection to this case. They are good at what they do. I had to overlook their tactics on some cases, but they're good men on the right side of the law. These officers will make the cartel people look like boy scouts. To bring down the house of the devil, I need to summon some real demons. He dials a number, but the person doesn't answer and he doesn't leave a message. *I'll call back a little later.*

CHAPTER NINE

Detective White arrives safely back at the casino hotel in Tunica with his federal agent bodyguards in tow. As he hands his car keys to the valet, he spots the uniformed man who had been following them. He is talking to Mary in the hotel lobby! *Well, now.* After a brief conversation, the two go their separate ways—Mary to the elevator and the man toward the stairs. *He's going right where I want him. I'll catch up with Mary later.* Paul goes into the stairwell soon after the man and catches up to him, tackling him to the ground. He pulls out his revolver and points it at the man's head. "I want to know who told you to follow me?"

"I don't know what you're talking about." Paul hits the man in the head with the butt of his gun.

"If you don't tell me who you are and why you're following me, I will blow your fucking head off. You better start talking."

By this time, the agents who are guarding Paul catch up with him, and the man realizes there isn't a way out, so he talks. "I was sent by someone in the DA's office. I don't know his name; I just know him as Boss. I don't know anything else, and that's the God's honest truth. Hell, I could lose my life over just telling you that."

"I could be the one who ends your life right here on these stairs, but I'm going to let my friends here take care of you. You're worth more alive than dead." He turns to the agents with a look of contempt in his eyes and says, "Can you deal with him?"

Agent Johnson, cupping his fist with his left hand, says, "Yeah, we'll take care of him. I'm sure Agent Woody would approve it." Johnson makes the necessary arrangements. "Another agent is coming to take him to headquarters."

The men head toward the lobby of the casino hotel. As they are walking, Paul decides to try his buddy in Chicago again. Taking his cell phone out of this pocket, he calls his friend, Detective Larry Newsome, a retired police officer. "Good morning, Larry. It's Paul."

"Paul, how are you? I haven't heard from you in a while. How's retirement?"

"Retirement is good. What about you?"

"I'm bored as hell! You can only watch so much TV."

Paul bursts out laughing. "Well, I have something for you that's right up your alley."

"Talk to me."

"I'm involved in a murder investigation of three, now four, of my classmates in Helena, Arkansas, that involves drugs and sex trafficking. I was thinking you and the guys could come down to help me and the FBI bring the cartel down."

Detective Newsome is eager to help. "Paul, I'll call the guys, and we'll drive down today. We'd never get past TSA at the airport with our travel gear. We'll touch base in the morning."

Paul chuckles and says, "Okay. Try not to drive too much over the limit. See you tomorrow."

As Paul heads toward the elevator to go to Mary's room, one of the henchmen reports to the Boss about what has transpired. "Hey Boss, I just saw two men take away one of our guys. They looked like the Feds. What do you want me to do?" The boss asks him if he was sure that it was their guy. "Boss, I'm positive it was him. He was handcuffed."

"Damn those Feds! I'm going to have to get the group together to determine how to proceed."

Later that morning, the council is on a conference call with the Boss. "I have called you all to inform you we have a problem. The Feds are involved. They've been trying to bring us down, but we have managed to stay a step ahead until now."

One of the members speaks up. "Don't lose your cool. We have things under control. A plan is in place to get rid of Detective White. We'll move up the time frame for his demise."

"Won't that put more suspicion on us from the Feds?"

"We don't pay you to question us. You're part of the reason we're in this position now. It was your man who killed Al Jennings before questioning him. You have no room to question us when your men are messing up. And because you can't find good help, we had to take care of that situation."

"Yes, sir, I understand. I'll keep you informed."

CHAPTER TEN

Mary has made it back to her room and is concerned about seeing her comrade chased by Paul. The ringing of her cell phone interrupts her thoughts. "Hello?"

"Mary, it's time to make that problem we discussed go away."

She sighs and says, "Okay. I'll let you know when I have taken care of the problem." She disconnects from the call and prepares for what she has to do.

A little while later, Paul knocks on her door. She looks at herself in the mirror, dressed in a sexy negligee, then goes to door, pausing to take a deep breath and put a smile on her face before opening it. As Paul enters her room, she says, "Paul, how was your trip?"

Paul is speechless for a moment as he looks at Mary in her negligee. "Good. I got what I needed, but before going to my hotel, I wanted to check on you."

"Well, what do you think?" She strikes a sexy pose.

Paul walks toward her and gathers her in his arms. He says, "Nice," then touches his lips to hers. When he breaks off the kiss, he says, "I'm going to take a quick shower and then you can greet me properly."

"Don't be too long, Paul." He goes into the bathroom, and Mary makes herself a drink at the bar. Just as she gets settled in bed, Paul comes out of the bathroom with only a towel wrapped around his waist. When he gets to the bed, he drops the towel and joins her in bed, where they make love into the night.

A few hours later, Mary is wide awake thinking about the problem she has to take care of. She tries not to wake Paul, but he stirs. "I'll be right back. Just going to the bathroom."

"Okay." When Mary gets up from the bed, Paul turns on his back and stretches. While he's stretching, his hand flips one of Mary's pillows and he notices a gun. *Hmm...* He puts the pillow back in place and thinks about their lovemaking session. Too bad nothing will come of this interlude. His thoughts are interrupted when Mary opens the bathroom door. She gets back into bed, and they turn toward each other and begin to kiss. Mary breaks off the kiss. "You've given me so much pleasure, Paul, but I can't take any pleasure in what I have to do." She reaches under her pillow for the gun and aims it at Paul.

"What the hell?! My lovemaking wasn't that bad, was it?"

"You were great, and that makes my job a little harder to do. If I didn't have any feelings for you, you would have been dead by now. I came here to do a job, and you're in the way. It's not personal." She pulls the trigger three times, but when nothing happens, she looks at Paul with a look of disbelief and fear. Paul reaches for his gun and says, "This is personal." He shoots her.

Frantic knocks from the door to the connecting room are heard. He gets up and pulls on a pair of pants and goes to the door. He holds his gun up and asks, "Who is it?

"It's Agent Johnson, Detective White. We heard everything."

Did they hear us making love? Paul lowers his gun and opens the door. The agents rush in. Paul explains what happened and then tentatively asks, "When you said you heard everything, how much did you hear?"

Agent Johnson replies, "We've had her room bugged since the day you all went to John Salon's house. We couldn't tell you about it ahead of time." Although Paul was not pleased to hear that, he understood. "We have to get you out of here fast. A team will come in and take care of the body and clean up the mess."

Paul goes back into the bedroom suite to gather his things and put on a shirt. As he leaves, he looks at Mary lying in a pool of blood on the bed and shakes his head. He and the detectives leave the room.

CHAPTER ELEVEN

The next morning, Paul awakens in a Memphis hotel where the FBI could keep an eye on him. He sits up on the side of the bed thinking about yesterday's events. He couldn't believe Mary had been hired to kill him. It had been years since he had to kill someone with his gun. It was all in the line of duty, but killing Mary was personal. He should have known their chance meeting in Tunica, of all places, was more than a coincidence. The ringing of his phone interrupted his thoughts. "Good morning, Larry."

"We're here."

"Great."

"Before we left Chicago, I spoke with a close friend of mine who is an agent with the DEA. He told me Percy Garcia and Raymond Shield are the real muscle of the cartel. They were part of the Colombian drug cartel in South America before they were kicked out. There is no love lost there. That is why they came to Arkansas. They wanted to build their own cartel in the States."

"Well, things are escalating here. They need to be taken

out. Once they're gone, everything else will fall into place. You know what to do. Let me know when it's complete." He hangs up.

Later that day, Raymond Shield and Percy Garcia are killed in a car explosion. Two days later, the Boss's dead body is found floating beneath a barge on the Mississippi River. Paul learned that he had been Detective Carl Woodson. His friends from Chicago were back home by now. Sometimes you have to take things into your own hands. A knock on the door told him it was time to leave for the FBI headquarters.

White and the two agents enter the building and head to the office of Agent Woody. As Paul and the agents enter the room, he notices there are several others in the room. Agent Woody comes around the table and greets him with a handshake. When the agent gets back to his seat, he says, "Great job, everyone! We have successfully solved these murders and taken down the cartel. Detective White, we would not have been able to get these indictments without your help. The department is indebted to you."

Detective White is humbled. He looks at Agent Woody and asks, "Are you sure you have enough evidence to bring down the cartel?"

"Paul, the DVDs were enough to indict District Attorney James Madison, and he has agreed to testify against the cartel and its operation as part of a plea deal. I'm not sure how the Columbians found Garcia and Shield, but they did us a huge favor. We can only assume they took care of the local boss as well." Woody jokes, "White, did you have something to do with that as well?" Everyone laughs, including White.

"David, you know me," he says, still laughing.

"Yes, I do. That's why I asked." Growing serious, Paul just returns the stare.

Agent Woody continues, "We also know why your three

friends were murdered. Due to your investigation, we also have a second key witness. This witness knows the entire operation of the cartel. Let me bring him in." He picks up the phone and asks for the witness to be brought into the room.

When the door opens, Paul can't believe his eyes. It was John Salon. "I thought you were dead!"

Agent Woody tells him John and his family have been in hiding this whole time. He explains, "With John's help, we were able to find out what was going on with the cartel. According to the evidence that we have gathered, the cartel killed Joe Wilson because he discovered the barges at the docks of the Arkansas Power and Light plant. They were being used by the cartel to export illegal drugs, sending them up and down the Mississippi River. John and Joe Wilson also discovered that Joe's daughter, along with other young girls, was forced into illegal prostitution for the cartel. Somehow the cartel found out, and they made plans to kill your three friends. We faked John's death and placed him and his family in witness protection. Even with his testimony, we still didn't have enough to bring down the cartel."

At this point, John speaks up. "I was scared for my life because I knew these people were dangerous. I must be honest; I didn't completely trust the agent I had contacted at the FBI. I assumed everyone was corrupt. I fully expected to be found dead or never found at all. That's why I left that box, Paul. I thought of that box daily. I was mad at myself for not sending the letter sooner. Honestly, I only had faith in one man," John says, pointing at Detective White. "He's never let me down."

The room remains silent until Agent Woody speaks. "Paul, according to the other sources, Dr. Mary Johnson was a top assassin for the cartel. She was also charged with cleaning up crime scenes for them."

Paul is about to speak before being interrupted by the receptionist on the intercom. "Sir, federal Judge Johnny Jones is on the line."

"Put him through." After a brief moment, Agent Woody says into the phone, "Judge Jones, I hope you have good news for me." He listens and then answers, "Great, and thanks again, Judge." He hangs up the phone and makes another call, saying, "It's time to move in on the remaining members of the cartel."

The FBI arrest several members of the cartel, including Phillips County municipal judge Carrington Beasley, who they later found out controlled the entire Delta cartel. Judge Beasley, it was later revealed, was so arrogant and confident in the cartel's control over the area that he ordered his hitmen to carve his initials on the chests of every hit he authorized. The hitmen were placed in federal custody.

* * * *

The next day, Detective White stands on top of a hill overlooking the Mississippi River with John Salon. Paul says, "What a beautiful sight, John. I hate to leave this place. I can't believe Joe, Jerry and Al are dead."

John replies, "You are still a humble man. Paul, without you, this case would still be open. More drugs would have been sold, innocent girls would still be forced into prostitution for these sickos, the police and other authorities would still be corrupt, and I would still be in hiding wondering when I would be next. I don't know how you did it, man, but you found the box that was meant for you. It must have been divine intervention." John looks down, shaking his head. "Paul, it was you that ended this madness. You are my hero."

White did not want to be the hero; he just wanted

justice to be served. Acting as if John had said nothing, Paul remains humble, as he always does when he closes a case. They stand in silence for a moment before Paul says, "I'll be leaving tomorrow for New York and getting back to a life of retirement."

"Hey, my brother, thank you for coming. I will be forever grateful to you."

"You're welcome."

Both men shake hands and walk down the hill to their cars. Before they part, John tells Paul, "Don't be a stranger."

UNNECESSARY MURDER IN THE FIRST DEGREE

A DETECTIVE PAUL WHITE
MYSTERY #2

CHAPTER ONE

Charles Turner is driving his 18-wheeler along the stretch of I-49 in Arkansas on his way home to Memphis, singing "The Thrill is Gone" along with B.B. King. He's not far from the small town of Marvell when a tire blows on his rig.

"The thrill is gone, baby. The thrill is gone ... what the hell?!"

He's able to pull his truck to the shoulder of the highway and exit the cab to investigate the damage. He grumbles to himself as he realizes he is going to have to change a tire. Since he's a professional, he has all he needs. It doesn't take him long, and he gets settled back in the cab when something catches his eye in the grass.

Is that someone sleeping in the grass? He remembers when he was homeless and reaches for a blanket to give to the stranger. As he gets closer to the person, he realizes the body is charred from burning. "Holy smokes!" He goes back to his truck and calls 911.

"911, what's your emergency?"

"I'm on Highway 49 going north about five miles outside

of Marvell, and there's a burned body underneath this overpass."

"Okay, sir. I'll send someone to check it out. Please stay where you are until they arrive."

"Okay," he tells the operator and hangs up. About 15 minutes later, a Phillips County sheriff's car arrives. Charles gets out of his truck and meets the deputy. "I called in about the burned body."

"Can you show me where you found the body?" Charles takes the deputy to the body and asks, "Can I get on my way now that you are here?"

"Afraid not. I have a few questions, and I need to call this in to the department."

Soon after, the scene gets roped off and several people are combing the grass for evidence and taking pictures of the scene. Charles has answered the deputy's questions and is sent on his way. Deputy Roy Fuller approaches Henry Bates, the medical examiner. "This is the third body to be found in the last two months."

"I know; it's quite troubling. Four teenaged black boys killed. This one was burned just like the last young man. When I do the autopsy, I'll be able to determine if there are any other similarities between the two."

"The last thing we need is a serial killer on the loose. People are upset about these deaths, but we don't have any leads. Whoever did this knows what they're doing. We do know that the others weren't killed where their bodies were found," Deputy Fuller says.

"I'm headed back to the morgue to get started. I'll let you know what I find."

* * * *

The next day, word gets out about another body being found. The Black community is fed up and has begun to protest in front of City Hall, demanding answers to these murders. The mayor is on the phone with Sheriff Bob Franklin.

"Bob, what's going on with this investigation? There are protestors outside my office demanding answers. Do we have a serial killer on our hands or not?"

"Mayor, I don't have any answers to give you. It looks like the work of a serial killer, but we haven't found any evidence to break the case. We are short on resources. Normally we have about 10 deputies, but I only have six to cover the county. I don't have the manpower. The cases are open, and we are working on them. Because the victims weren't killed where they were found, it is making it real hard to find out what happened. Believe me, we are doing our best. Let me check with the medical examiner and see how he's coming with the autopsy."

"We definitely don't need word getting out if you think this is the work of a serial killer. Our peaceful town has been turned upside down with these murders. That news will take people over the edge. Keep me posted."

As soon as the sheriff hangs up, his phone rings again. "Sheriff Franklin."

"Bob, I've completed the autopsy on the young man found yesterday. He was partially burned and strangled like Michael Dickerson. We were able to identify him. It's Aaron Chamberlain."

"Aaron?! He's supposed to be at camp. Are you sure?"

"Yes. I was thrown for a loop when I realized it. The birthmark on the back of his calf was visible."

"He wasn't castrated, was he?"

"No, he wasn't."

"Thank God! How am I going to break this news to my cousin? She's going to be devastated."

"I know. I wanted to let you know right away. I have to finish up the autopsy, but I'll let you know if I find anything else."

"Okay, and thanks, Henry." The sheriff hangs up and sits back in his chair wondering how he will tell his cousin. *It's days like this when I hate my job. We need a break in these cases soon.* He gets up to leave to deliver the news to his cousin.

CHAPTER TWO

L ife has settled down in Marvell. It has been four months since the body of Aaron Chamberlain was found with no new leads. One day, Wallace Green was fishing along the banks of the Mississippi when he noticed something floating in the river that looked like a body. He wasn't sure what he saw, so he dismissed it until he saw a second, similar form floating in the river. This one looked bloated, so he called 911. *There goes a peaceful day,* he thought to himself as he was speaking to the operator.

Soon the shore was abuzz with activity. It was confirmed that those were bodies Wallace had seen floating. While the deputies were retrieving the bodies, another one was found for a total of three bodies in the same day. Deputy Fuller is talking to Sheriff Franklin on shore.

"Sheriff, looks like things are about to get crazy again. We've never had this many murders in such a short period of time. As a matter of fact, I don't remember hearing anything about this many murders in our town's history! What is going on?"

"I know. And this is really looking like the work of a serial killer. First the four black boys are found dead. Now three white boys have the same fate. There has to be a connection because this makes no sense. We'll see what the M.E. finds in the autopsies."

"We need a break before the murderer decides to strike again. Let's hope this doesn't turn into something racial."

"That's the last thing we need. I'm going to talk to the M.E. and then head back to the office."

The sheriff approaches Dr. Bates. "Henry, how soon do you think you can be done with the autopsies?"

"It's going to take me a few days. Their throats were cut, but we'll have to see what else turns up."

"So far, we don't have any leads. Let me know if you find anything else." Sheriff Franklin turns and walks toward his cruiser.

* * * *

Back at his office, Sheriff Franklin is puzzled by these murders and realizes he is going to need some help. *Who can I call? Paul White. Yes!* The sheriff and Paul, a retired detective from the Chicago Police Department, have been friends for years. He recently helped solve some murders in Helena, Arkansas, that had very little evidence. *He's the person I need.* Sheriff Franklin picks up his phone to call his friend.

"Paul, Bob Franklin. How are you?"

"Hey, Bob! I haven't heard from you in a while. How are you?"

"I could be better. How have you been doing? Is New York treating you well?"

"I've been doing just fine, enjoying retirement. What's going on with you? Are Ella and the kids doing okay?"

"They're doing great. Ella has been on me about eating healthier. But my reason for calling you today is work related. I need your help."

"What's going on?"

"Paul, I have some major problems here. In the last six months, we have had seven teenaged boys murdered. Four of them are black, and three are white. My cousin, Aaron, was one of the boys murdered, Paul. The townspeople are getting restless, and this looks like the work of a serial killer."

"I'm sorry to hear about your cousin and the other boys. What can I do?"

"Come out of retirement for an old friend and help me solve these cases."

"Sure." He smiles, thinking how satisfying it is to help people, especially his old friends. "What do you know so far?"

"My deputies and I have been running into brick walls in our investigation. None of the boys were killed where we found them, so there hasn't been any substantial evidence. Two of the black boys were strangled and their bodies were partially burned; the other two black boys were shot execution style. The three white boys had their throats cut and were just found in the Mississippi, all on the same day. Paul, people are afraid and angry, rightfully so. I need a break in these cases, and I think you're the man who can find it."

"Bob, you caught me at a good time. I can be down there by the end of the week."

"Thanks, Paul. Let me know when you arrive." He hangs up the phone, feeling a lot better that Detective Paul White is now on the case.

CHAPTER THREE

A few days later, Paul is leaving the Memphis airport in a rental car for Marvell. He calls Sheriff Franklin. "Bob, I'm headed your way."

"Okay, see you soon, Paul." Sheriff Franklin then calls the desk clerk. "Eileen, can you have Deputies Fuller and Fox come to my office?"

"Yes, sir."

A few minutes later, the deputies walk into his office. "Sheriff, you wanted to see us?" Deputy Fuller asks.

"Yes, I want you all to go back out to that overpass and see if there is anything we might have missed."

"Uh, Sheriff, it's been months since we found that body. Do you really think anything is out there?" Deputy Fuller asks.

"Maybe, maybe not, but I need something to break these cases open. So go out and take another look."

"Okay," Deputy Fuller says. "Let's go Fox."

Across the street, someone has been watching the sheriff's office through binoculars and sees the deputies leave. *Hmm, where are they going? Deputy Fuller is the lead on those murders. Maybe he has discovered something new.* The Shadow walks briskly to his car and follows the deputies.

A couple of hours later, Detective White arrives at the Phillips County Sheriff's Office. He walks in, stopping at the clerk's desk. "I'm here to see Sheriff Franklin."

"Are you Paul White?" Mrs. Smith asks.

"Yes, I am."

"He's expecting you. Let me page him." She picks up the phone. "Sheriff, Paul White is here."

"Okay. I'll be right out, Eileen."

"Mr. White, the sheriff will be with you shortly."

A few minutes later, Sheriff Franklin comes out of his office and greets Detective White.

"Hot damn, old buddy! I'm sure happy as hell that you made it. I'm glad you could come down to help me out."

"No problem, Bob. I was a little bored anyway. This will keep me busy for a while."

"Great! Let's go into my office so I can bring you up to date." The sheriff and Paul enter his office. "Have a seat. Man, I can't tell you how relieved I am to see you. I sent two of my deputies to the location where one of the bodies was found. I know it's been a while since he was found, but maybe our guys missed something. I'm pulling at straws here."

"I understand. What have you got?"

While the sheriff updates Paul, Deputies Fuller and Fox are searching the area near Highway 49. Unbeknownst to them, the Shadow is watching them from the overpass. As the deputies begin their search, Deputy Fuller says, "You start up top and work your way down, and I'll start from the bottom, working my way up."

"Okay. Do you think we'll find anything?" Deputy Fox asks.

"I don't know, but it won't hurt to look. Bag up anything you see that might help the case. Let's get this over with and then get something to eat."

Deputy Fuller stands at the sight where Aaron's body was found. *If ever we needed someone to talk from the grave, it's right now.* He begins walking methodically from left to right, working his way toward Deputy Fox, when something catches his eye. He stoops down and moves the grass away.

"Fox! Come here!"

Just as Deputy Fox arrives, Deputy Fuller stands up, holding a partially burned card in his gloved hand.

"What's that?"

"It looks like some kind of identification card. Let me bag it up. Did you find anything?"

Fox answers, "No. Do you think that card belongs to one of the murderer?"

"I hope so because we need a break in these cases. Let's continue looking and then take this to the lab."

As the deputies continue their search, the Shadow becomes concerned after seeing Fuller put something in an evidence bag. *What did he find? It's been months since that boy was found. There couldn't be any evidence left at the scene.* Continuing to watch the deputies, he says out loud, "I may have to kill again."

CHAPTER FOUR

D etective White is in his hotel room thinking about the murders. He opens the file of Michael Dickerson, one of the black teenagers. There isn't much evidence. None of the victims were killed where they were found, but they were all naked. Two of the boys were castrated, and Paul wonders if this is the work of a pedophile. But there is no evidence of other sexual activity with any of the victims. Paul worked a few serial killer cases in Chicago, and it wasn't easy solving them. It took months, and one case took over a year to solve.

He continues to look through the file when a small, partially burned piece of paper falls onto the floor. *Did they miss this?* To read what's on the paper, he puts on his reading glasses, but he can't make out the writing clearly. *I need some new glasses.* He pulls out his magnifying glass and determines that it is a ticket stub from Amtrak.

He immediately calls Bob. "Bob, Paul. I was going through the file of Michael Dickerson and a partially burned piece of paper fell out of the file. From what I can tell, it's an Amtrak ticket."

"How did my guys miss that?"

"It was probably stuck between some papers in the file."

"Can you bring that in tomorrow? One of my deputies found a partially burned card at the scene, under the bridge, where the Black boys were found. We can have both analyzed."

"Yes, I can bring it in, but I was thinking about sending this ticket stub to the FBI lab in Virginia. I can also send the piece of evidence your deputies found."

"That sounds like a great idea. This might be the break we need, Paul. I'll see you first thing in the morning."

* * * *

The next morning in Sheriff Franklin's office, Paul and Deputies Fox and Fuller are gathered.

"Guys, Detective White found a partially burned Amtrak ticket stub last night when he was going through Dickerson's file. He wants to send it to the FBI lab in Virginia along with the identification card you found yesterday."

"Could this be the break we need?" Deputy Fuller asks.

"I hope so, but I don't want to get too excited."

Paul says, "I have come to the conclusion that these murders are related and are the work of a serial killer. I don't want to get my hopes up too much until I hear back from the lab. I can contact a relative who is an agent with the FBI to get this pushed though, especially since we don't have any other leads."

"That would be great, Paul," Sheriff Franklin says.

Outside, the Shadow is leaning against a pole looking in the direction of the Sheriff's office. *Those deputies found something yesterday and that sheriff has called in help from an outsider, Detective Paul White.* He overheard his name at the diner yesterday when he and the sheriff were having lunch. *White could be a problem because the sheriff and his deputies can't find their way out of a bag.* He walks away.

In the sheriff's office, the meeting is coming to a close. Paul asks, "Bob, is it possible to go to the morgue to talk to the M.E. and take a look at the unidentified bodies?"

"Yes, let's go over there now. Fox and Fuller, you all can get back to work. I'll keep you posted."

Paul and Sheriff Franklin arrive at the morgue. The sheriff greets Dr. Bates. "Good morning, Henry. I would like to introduce you to a friend of mine, Detective Paul White. He's retired from the Chicago Police Department."

"Nice to meet you, Paul."

"The same here, Dr. Bates."

"Call me Henry. What can I do for you, Bob?"

"Paul wanted to know if you could reexamine the boys who haven't been identified."

"Sure, it's a slow day. You want to watch?"

Paul replies, "I haven't examined a body in a long time. Sure, I'll stay. Bob?"

"I'll stay as well."

"Great! Let me get everything set up; I'll be back."

When he's ready, Dr. Bates asks Bob and Paul to come into the room. There are two bodies on separate tables covered by a sheet.

Dr. Bates says, "The body to your right is the first boy we found, John Doe. The body on the left is the second body, John Doe 2. My initial autopsy concluded all of the victims were starved or at least given very little to eat before they were killed. John Doe hadn't eaten for one to two days based on the contents of his intestines. The same for John Doe 2. All of the victims have some sort of tattoo on their chest."

"Yes, I saw that in the files. Do you know what it represents?" Paul asks.

"We haven't determined that, but we think it could be a gang or religious sect," Sheriff Franklin replies.

Paul asks, "Henry, can I take a look at the tattoos?"

"Sure," he says, pulling back the sheet on John Doe.

Paul steps in for a closer look, but the tattoo doesn't look familiar to him. "It's definitely related to some type of group because they are all the same. I also noticed the indentations on the backs of a couple of the boys."

"Yes, those are from something heavy on their backs. Probably the killer was holding them down with his knee while he strangled them."

Paul shakes his head, thinking about what the victims had to suffer at the hands of their killer. "It's a shame what happened to these boys."

"I know," says Henry. "In the clothing of all the boys were small pieces of leaves that didn't come from the murder scene. They are from a sugar maple tree."

"So, we know they had all been held in the same location, but where?" the sheriff asks. "That's what we need to find out."

"And who killed them," Paul reminds him.

"Henry, thank you for taking time out of your day to go over the results with us. Your autopsies are very thorough, so there's no need at this point to ask you to do them again or send the bodies off to a lab."

"Let me know if you need me for anything else, Bob. Though I don't mind the work, I wish I didn't have to be so busy with these cases. I'll be glad when everything is solved, and we can get back to normal."

"Yeah, I know what you mean. We're going to send some evidence to the FBI lab, and hopefully, that will give us the break we've needed."

"Good luck. It was nice meeting you, Paul."

"Same here, Henry."

CHAPTER FIVE

Paul and Bob return to the sheriff's office.

"Let me call the FBI agent I was telling you about. He's a cousin by marriage. His brother works for the police department in Helena."

Paul pulls out his cell phone and calls his cousin. "Good morning, may I speak with Agent Bruce Hamilton?"

"Hamilton."

"Bruce, this is Paul White. How are you?"

"Paul! Good to hear from you, man. I'm doing well. How have you been?"

"Enjoying retirement, but right now, I'm helping the sheriff in Marvell with seven murder cases."

"That's down in my brother Mike's neck of the woods. He told me about the murders. Damn shame."

Paul briefs Bruce about the murders and how there haven't been any leads. He tells him he has some evidence that needs processing and asks if the FBI lab can process it for him.

"I can see why you came out of retirement to help solve this case. I can get the evidence rushed through the lab for you. I'll email the information you need to send the evidence."

"Thank you, Bruce. I owe you one."

"Now that I know you come out of retirement periodically, I might take you up on that. You did a great job with those murders in Helena."

"Thank you. I wish I didn't have to come out of retirement to do this, but once a cop, always a cop," Paul says to Bruce. "Again, thanks for your help, and I will send the evidence off as soon as I get the information. About how long do you think it will take to get results?"

"I'm not sure because it depends on the evidence and what they can extract from it, but I would hope within the next two weeks."

"Okay, Bruce, talk to you later." He disconnects and says to Bob, "He said we should hear something within the next two weeks, but the lab can make a better determination once they receive the evidence."

"Well, we'll wait until we hear from the lab."

"I'm going to head back to my hotel and hit the slots. When I hear from Bruce, I'll call you."

"I'll have Eileen send the evidence. Take care, and I'll talk to you soon."

When Paul exits the Sheriff's office, the Shadow straightens up from his position and heads to his car to follow Detective White. As Paul is crossing the bridge over the Mississippi, he notices the Shadow's car has been following him for several miles. Paul speeds up and checks his passenger-side mirror to see if the car speeds up too. It does. He's not far from the casino and soon pulls into the first parking lot he sees.

The Shadow keeps driving down the road and ends up at a large acreage of cotton. *It's time to step up my game. Paul White doesn't know who he's messing with, but he's going to find out.*

CHAPTER SIX

Three weeks later, Detective Paul White is in Sheriff Franklin's office about to go over the results from the FBI lab. "I wasn't sure if they would be able to find out anything from that ticket, but I was hopeful. The report says the train ticket was bought in Baltimore, Maryland."

"Really?" the sheriff asks.

"It was bought for Russell Roberts and the identification card belongs to Elliot Murray."

Relief appears on the sheriff's face, and his shoulders relax as he hears Paul read the names.

"I knew bringing you in on these cases was going to help. What else is in the report?"

"Bruce included information regarding the missing person's reports for both boys. They were from the Baltimore area and were attending a camp outside the city called Camp Archmore when they went missing. They have been missing for almost two years."

"Two years! Whoever did this is facing charges of kidnapping and murder. And because they crossed state lines, the Feds are going to be involved."

"Yeah. Bruce said that would happen, and he would like to get whatever information we have so far."

"I can do one better. I can send Fuller and Fox. They have been investigating all the murders. Let me have Eileen locate them." He picks up the phone and calls the desk clerk.

Half hour later, Deputies Fuller and Fox enter the sheriff's office; Sheriff Franklin asks them to have a seat.

"We got the report back from the FBI lab, and this case has blown wide open." He goes on to update the deputies. "I'm going to need y'all to go to Baltimore to help the local police and Feds as soon as possible. How soon can you leave?"

"Sir, Laura is due in about two weeks, and I really don't want to leave right now, but these cases have been bothering me. Do you know how long we might be gone?

"I can't give you that answer. Family is important; if you need to stay close to home, I understand, Fox."

"I want to see this through to the end. I know it's important for me to be by Laura's side when she gives birth, but it's not like it's our first. This baby will be number three. We'll have to move some things around, but I can be ready to leave in a couple of days."

"My wife can help out while you are gone."

"I appreciate that, Sheriff. I'll talk to Laura and see what she needs."

"What about you Fuller?"

"I don't have anything pressing; I can be ready when Fox is."

"Great. I really appreciate you all doing this. I'll send you the contact information for the detective in Baltimore. We're going to be short on staff, so I'll call the sheriff in Madison County to see if he can spare someone while you're gone."

* * * *

Later that day, the sheriff and Paul are having dinner at the diner when Judge Thomas Andrew walks up to their table.

"Bob, how are you?"

"I'm doing good, Judge. This is my friend Paul White. He's helping me with those murder cases," Bob says. "Paul, this is retired Judge Thomas Andrew."

"Nice to meet you," Paul says.

"Same here. I'm glad you're able to help with the cases. Bob hasn't had any breaks, but he's been doing a wonderful job with what he's got."

"We're hoping to get a break soon and hopefully close out these cases," Sheriff Franklin says.

"Gentlemen, I don't want to bother you any longer. I just came in to pick up an order. Detective White, it was good to meet you. Bob, take care."

After the judge has moved away, Paul says, "You didn't tell him I was a detective."

"He probably just assumed you were since you're helping me with these cases."

Paul wasn't totally convinced but let it go for now.

* * * *

Two days later, the deputies enter the Baltimore Police Department and walk up to the desk sergeant.

"Good morning. We're here to see Detective Ray Hatfield about the missing boys from the camp. We are Deputies Fuller and Fox from Arkansas."

"Yes, he's expecting you. Have a seat, and I'll let him know you're here."

A few minutes later, Detective Hatfield approaches the deputies. "I'm Detective Hatfield. I'm glad you all could make it. Let's go into my office so we can talk."

Once everyone is seated, the detective begins speaking. "Again, thank you for coming all this way to assist us. Your sheriff sent me copies of your files, which has been very helpful."

"You're welcome," Fuller says. "We've been looking for a break in these cases for months, and we finally got it with the help of our sheriff's friend."

"Yes, Paul White. He's a good man and good at what he does. I learned a lot from him when I worked for the Chicago Police Department. He solved a lot of cases in Chicago."

"He has been a huge help to these cases," Fuller says.

"Wow! I can understand why the townspeople are in an uproar. Things like this don't usually happen in small towns. Let me tell you about the investigation on our end."

The detective tells the deputies that the identification card belonged to 16-year-old Elliott Murray from Baltimore. They were able to match his fingerprints to ones retrieved from the boy's home. The second boy, Russell Roberts, was 15 years old from Annapolis, Maryland. They were able to positively identify him from fingerprints from his home as well. They also had footage of him at the Amtrak station on his way to the camp.

"So they were taken from camp, held in an unknown location, killed who-knows-where and their bodies dumped in Marvell?" Fox asks.

"That seems to be the case," Detective Hatfield says, explaining, "Elliott and Russell were with their unit hiking a trail. The camp counselor said when the group was eating lunch on the trail, the boys wandered off and never came back. They looked for them for several days but, obviously, didn't find them. We've already told the families, and they're making preparations for their funerals."

Fuller said, "It's good to know four of the seven boys

have been identified. The two boys from our area, Aaron and Michael, had been at camp as well, but one located in Tennessee."

"I saw that. The camp in Tennessee is affiliated with Camp Archmore. The headquarters is here in Baltimore, but they have camps in just about every state. They have an affiliation with a church. We can head over there now." They all leave the office.

* * * *

The Shadow, through a source, found out that the Arkansas deputies were traveling to Baltimore for the case. He needed to come to headquarters anyway, so he decided to follow them to Baltimore.

CHAPTER SEVEN

At the Camp Archmore national headquarters, the detective and deputies are talking to the president of the organization, John Goodman.

"Good morning, Mr. Goodman. I'm Detective Hatfield, and these are Deputies Roy Fuller and Michael Fox from Arkansas. We are here concerning the deaths of Russell Roberts and Elliott Murray who were at Camp Archmore outside Baltimore when they disappeared."

"Yes, I was so sorry to hear about that. We have never had anything like this happen at our camps, so this was truly a surprise. We are at your service. What can I do for you, Detective?" Goodman asks.

"We would like to talk to someone who came in contact with the boys while they were at camp."

"Our personnel director, Betty Green, will be able to help you. She should be in shortly."

"Great," Detective Hatfield said. "We'll wait."

"You can wait for her in the conference room down the hall. I'll take you there."

* * * *

The Shadow is standing by a tree in the parking lot of the camp headquarters. He saw the detective and deputies go in earlier. He's getting anxious because he knows he's going to be found out. Something catches his eye to the right; he looks over and sees Betty Green getting out of her car. He walks toward her.

"Good morning, Betty. How have you been doing?"

Betty replies, "Just fine. How have you been doing? It's been a while since I've seen you."

"Let me walk you to your office. Here, let me help you carry those."

"That would be great, thanks. I've got to put something in storage before I go to my office. Follow me."

To get to the storage area, they use a side entrance and then get on an elevator. Once they exit the elevator, they walk down the hall to the storage area. The Shadow pulls out a gun with a silencer from his jacket and aims it at Betty.

Betty is none the wiser as she tells him, "The door is at the end of the hall."

As she turns her head to look at the Shadow, he shoots her three times. Betty falls to the ground, and the Shadow heads back out of the building the way he came in.

* * * *

Meanwhile, back in Marvell, Sheriff Franklin and Detective White are discussing the case.

"Paul, I bet the three white boys we haven't been able to identify attended a camp associated with the others."

"You're probably right on that point."

Paul goes back to looking at one of the files of the white teenaged boys. *Maybe we missed something.* As he's turning over a page in the file, he notices two pages stuck together.

"Bob, these pages are stuck together in this file. I missed it the first time I went through it, and it looks like there's something between them."

Paul separates the papers and sees a torn piece of paper. Before the sheriff can say something, his phone rings. "Sheriff Franklin."

"Sheriff, it's Fuller."

"Hey, let me put you on speaker so Detective White can hear. He and I were just going over notes on the cases again. How are things going in Baltimore?"

"The personnel director was killed while we were waiting on her to arrive to work today. The director had said she would be able to give us the names of the people who had contact with the boys at camp."

"I don't think that's a coincidence. We must be getting close, and someone knows their time is up."

"We agree. She was seen going into a side entrance of the building with a man, but we can't identify him because he was holding his head down. There are no cameras where she was found. The camera outside the door shows him leaving and that's it."

"He's the killer," Paul said. "Do you know if there have been any more missing person reports for other attendees of the camps?"

"We're looking into it," Fuller said.

"I hate to hear about another life being taken, but this case is about to be blown wide open. Keep me updated, and I will do the same." He disconnects the call. "Paul, we're finally making some headway."

* * * *

In Baltimore, the Shadow is sitting in a restaurant across the street from the camp headquarters. *I need to get into Betty's files to make sure my name isn't mentioned. I hope my badge still works.*

Later that night, the Shadow walks across the street to the headquarters. He gets his badge out of his pocket and holds it up to the scanner. He holds his breath until he sees the green light then opens the door. When he gets to Betty's office, the door is locked. He rattles the doorknob, frustrated. He slams his hand against the door and screams.

He paces back and forth in front of the office. *I need to see those files.* He realizes there is nothing he can do about it tonight, so he leaves the building and goes back to the restaurant.

The next day, a teenage boy is found dead in the alley behind the restaurant across from the camp headquarters.

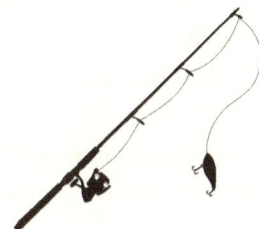

CHAPTER EIGHT

In the sheriff's office, Paul and Bob examine the piece of paper.

"What is it?" the sheriff asks.

"It looks like a piece of vellum. Dr. Bates found it in one of the boys' stomach during the autopsy. There's some writing on it, but we will have to send it to the lab."

"I don't understand how this was overlooked. This could help open the case. Let's send it off." The sheriff's phone rings, and he answers it.

"Bob, this is Henry. I was looking at one of the boys again and came across something I missed."

"And Paul and I just discovered something that was overlooked in one of the files. What did you find?"

"I discovered a piece of plastic in his stomach that appears to be a part of a driver license. The only thing visible is the driver's license number."

"Bag it up for me, Henry, and I'll come get it right away."

When Bob and Paul return from the medical examiner's office, they run the license numbers through the system. Nothing comes back.

"Let's send the information to Baltimore. There's a connection somewhere," Paul says.

"Okay. I'm emailing it to Detective Hatfield now."

"Bob, I've been wondering if the person who did these killings lives in this area but is associated with those camps. Do you know anyone who could be associated with the camps?"

"No, not off the top of my head, but maybe that information I just sent will result in another break." He picks up his phone to make a call.

"Baltimore Police Department, how may I help you?"

"Detective Hatfield, please."

"One minute."

"Detective Hatfield."

"Detective, Sheriff Bob Franklin from Marvell."

"Hello, Bob. What can I do for you?"

"I just emailed you a picture of a partial driver's license. I wanted to make sure you received it."

"Let me check," he says. "Yes, I see it."

"Great! I couldn't find a match in our system, so I was hoping you might be able to find something."

"I'll check and let you know."

"Anything new on your end?"

"We're not sure if it's related, but a teenage boy was found murdered behind a restaurant that's across the street from the camp headquarters. We're going through the files of the personnel director now. I'll let you know what we find and get back to you about the ID."

* * * *

Detective Hatfield is running the ID numbers through the system while the deputies go through the personnel files.

Fox says, "I've come across someone who visits the camps regularly, Robert McAllister."

"That's who this driver's license number belongs to. What does his file say?"

"He is in charge of all the camp directors. He makes periodic visits to each camp."

"Really? His license says he was born in 1946. That makes him 76 years old. No way he does all that traveling at his age and committing seven, possibly eight, murders. I don't see it."

"Me either," Fox says. "I'll keep looking."

"Let me see what I can find on Robert McAllister."

A short while later, Detective Hatfield says, "McAllister lives 35 miles outside of Baltimore on a farm. There's a number for him. Let me call."

"Hello, I am looking for Robert McAllister."

"Mr. McAllister doesn't live here anymore. He's in a nursing home."

"I'm a detective with the Baltimore police, and I really need to talk to Mr. McAllister about a case. Who am I speaking with?"

"I'm just the housekeeper. I come in periodically to keep the house clean. I can give you Miss Carolyn's number. She's his daughter and lives in Forrest City, Arkansas. He has a son too, Albert, but no one has seen him in a long time. Miss Carolyn should be able to help you. Here's her number."

"Thank you. I will give her a call." He hangs up and says to the deputies, "Can you all see what you can find out about Carolyn McAllister and Albert McAllister in Forrest City, Arkansas?"

Fuller says, "I can have the sheriff look into it." He calls Sheriff Franklin.

* * * *

It doesn't take long for Sheriff Franklin to call Detective Hatfield back with information.

"Detective, I found some information on Carolyn and Albert. The McAllisters live in Madison County, the next county over from ours. She doesn't have a record, but Albert does. His crimes have been against children. He's registered as a sex offender, but his current location is unknown. I sent a deputy to his last known address, and he was told no one lived at that residence with that name."

"Sheriff, I'm going to give Carolyn a call and see what she can tell me."

* * * *

Carolyn McAllister's phone rings. "Hello?"

"May I speak with Carolyn McAllister?"

"This is she."

"Ms. McAllister, my name is Detective Hatfield from the Baltimore Police Department, and we are trying to locate your brother Albert."

"I haven't seen him in years, Detective."

"When was the last time you saw him?"

"About five years ago when we visited our father in Maryland."

"Ms. McAllister, we really need to find your brother because he is a person of interest in a case we're working."

"What did he do?"

"Seven teenaged boys were kidnapped from summer camp and killed."

"You think my brother killed those boys? He wouldn't do anything like that!"

"Ma'am, I didn't say he killed those young men. I said he is a person of interest. All the boys were found in Marvell,

Arkansas. Would it be okay if I had a local sheriff come out to your property to do a search?"

"If it will rule Albert out as a suspect, yes. What do I have to do?"

"I'll have the sheriff give you a call to set up a time. Thank you for your cooperation, and if you hear from your brother, please call me." He disconnects the call and calls Sheriff Franklin to update him.

Several hours later, a deputy and Detective White arrive at Carolyn McAllister's home.

* * * *

Now in Marvell, the Shadow is standing inside an old abandoned Baptist church looking out the windows, saying, "O Lord, thank you for giving me the power and the glory to purify mankind. I realize purification can only be done through the purification of young men. They are truly lost."

He turns to face the altar. The need to kill overcomes him as he exits the church.

At the McAllister home, the deputy rings the bell and Carolyn opens the door.

"Are you all here to search my property?"

"Yes, I'm Deputy Abe Jones from the Madison County Sheriff's Department, and this is Detective Paul White. We brought a canine with us. Do you mind if we get started?"

"No, go right ahead. Like I told the detective, I haven't seen my brother in years, so you're not going to find anything. But, suit yourself."

CHAPTER NINE

Paul and the deputy, in a section of the property far from the house, decide to let the dog loose to see if it picks up a trail.

"Looks like your dog is onto something, Abe. Let's go."

The dog heads toward the grounds of an abandoned Baptist church. They go through an old cemetery before coming to the building. The dog sits outside the door, anxious to get inside. When the Abe and Paul reach the door, they find it unlocked and go inside. The dog races to the back of the church and down some steps with the deputy and Paul close behind. The dog begins to bark and turns in a circle.

There are several rooms in the basement. As they open the doors, they discover a boy in each room. They encounter one boy with his hands tied and mouth gagged who is barely alive.

"Unbelievable," Deputy Jones says. "I've got to call this in."

He doesn't have any reception in the basement, so he goes outside the church to call his sheriff. He notices a fresh grave in the distance and relays this information. Soon the property is swarming with paramedics, sheriffs and deputies.

Sheriff Franklin asks Deputy Jones, "How many boys did you find downstairs?"

"A total of five, sir."

"Where did you see this grave?"

"Over here. Follow me."

As the graves are being dug up, Sheriff Franklin approaches Paul. "I'm glad we found those boys in time. But whoever put them there is not going to be happy."

"No, they aren't. I have a strange feeling ... like someone is watching us."

"Your instincts are usually spot on, but are you sure it's not because we're in a cemetery?"

"Cemeteries creep me out, but this is different. I bet we're being watched by the killer right now."

The Shadow peeks around a large oak tree looking through his binoculars at the commotion at the church. *They got lucky this time, but I will not be stopped because I'm on a mission for God.*

* * * *

A couple of days later, Sheriff Franklin and Paul are at the medical examiner's office. Two of the bodies in the grave had been sent there to expedite the autopsies.

Dr. Bates says, "Good morning, gentlemen. Albert McAllister is dead."

They both yell, "Dead?!"

"Yes, one of the two bodies I have is his."

"Well, we're back to square one," Sheriff Franklin says.

"Not so fast," Dr. Bates says. "The other body is that of Barry Moore from Tennessee. He wrote a letter and hid it in his clothes. Here it is." He continues as they look at the evidence, "He says he was kidnapped in his sleep while he was attending summer camp in Tennessee near Memphis. He mentions one of the camp instructors, Reverend Jimmy Whitehead."

"Reverend Whitehead wouldn't kill a fly. Plus, he has arthritis in his hands. He doesn't have the strength. But that was his old church where we found the boys."

"Bob, I know you know him, but we can't leave any stone unturned in this case. I told you yesterday, it felt like we were being watched."

"I know, Paul, but I just can't think that Whitehead could commit these murders."

"What about his family members?"

"Some of his family members have some skeletons in their closets. There is one person we can talk to about the Whitehead family, Beatrice Wilson. She was the Whitehead maid for about forty years. Mrs. Wilson is now living in a nursing home in West Helena. If there is anyone that would have knowledge concerning the Whitehead family, it would be her. We should talk with her immediately."

When the Sheriff and Detective White arrive at the nursing home, they are told that Beatrice is in the dining room, so they head that way. They find her at a table with another lady talking.

"Good morning, Mrs. Wilson, this is Detective White and I'm Sheriff Franklin. We are here to ask you some questions regarding the Whitehead family."

Mrs. Wilson says, "Good morning, Sheriff Franklin and Detective White. What exactly do you want know about the Whiteheads?"

"Beatrice, I'm going to go to my room. Come see me when you're finished."

"Okay, Ruth."

Sheriff Franklin says, "You worked for the family a long

time, and I know you were privy to a lot that went on in the household. There was a scandal years ago with the Reverend and his mistress. What do you know about that?"

"Now, Sheriff, I don't go around gossiping about people."

"I know, Mrs. Wilson, but this is important. Detective White and I are working on the case of those teenaged boys who were killed, and we think we are close to solving the crimes."

"I was so upset when I heard about the killings. Who would want to kill those boys?" she asks. "You don't think Reverend Whitehead did it, do you?"

"We're not sure, but we need to cover our bases."

"The Reverend couldn't kill anybody because of his arthritis."

"He could have someone do it for him," Paul says.

With a grimace she says, "You could be right on that point. When it came out about the mistress and the son she had by the Reverend, Mrs. Whitehead took to her bed. She was so embarrassed. I tried to tell her, but you know, people don't listen to the help."

The men nod, uncomfortably.

"Delores Dickerson was her name. She was from Elaine, Arkansas. After the scandal, she married a man from Helena, and they moved out of state."

"I'm from Helena. Do you know who she married?" Paul asks.

"No, I don't, but she gave birth to a boy in May 1975. His name is Justice Dickerson. The Reverend would get to see him every now and then, but then the visits stopped."

"Do you know where Delores got married?" Paul asks.

"She got married here in town by the justice of the peace. The Reverend found out about her getting married, and he wanted me to make sure she was really getting married. So

I stood outside the courthouse and saw her wearing a white dress and veil. That was proof enough for me, so I reported back to the Reverend."

"Paul, let's go to the license office to take a look at that marriage certificate. Mrs. Wilson, thank you for your help. We'll let you get on with your day."

"You're welcome, Sheriff. I hope you find who killed those boys soon."

* * * *

Paul and the Sheriff wait for the clerk to come back with the marriage license.

"Sheriff, here's the marriage license. Delores Dickerson married Reggie Andrew. I remember the day she came in to apply for the license. I was so happy because of that mess she got into with Reverend Whitehead. Do you know he wanted her to get an abortion? A man of the cloth asking a woman to do that, humph. I'm glad she changed that boy's last name."

"She changed her son's last name?" the Sheriff asks.

"Yes. She tried to get Reverend Whitehead to have a relationship with the boy. It worked for a while. She got fed up and asked the right reverend to give up his parental rights so her new husband could adopt the boy. She told him if he did that, he wouldn't hear from her or the boy again."

"So, the boy's name is Justice Andrew?"

"Yes. He had a rough childhood, getting in and out of trouble. He made it through high school and went to college, then to medical school. Delores is so proud of him. He gives a lot to different organizations, especially youth organizations."

"Do you know where he lives?" Sheriff Franklin asked.

"He's a medical examiner in Memphis."

Paul and Bob look at each other.

"Alice, thank you for your help. Take care."

Detective White and the Sheriff head back to Bob's office to call the medical examiner in Memphis. When they do, they find out that he is on vacation. Bob hangs up and tells Paul, "Justice Andrew is at the same camp where Barry Moore was kidnapped. Let's take a ride."

CHAPTER TEN

The Shadow is also at the camp in Tennessee watching the boys do their workout from a window in one of the buildings on the grounds. As he comes out of the building, he greets one of the campers. "Hey, Jordan. How are you?"

"I'm doing good, Dr. Andrew."

"Where are you going?"

"To archery."

"Have fun."

Just as the camper moves on, the Sheriff and Paul approach Justice Andrew.

"Dr. Andrew?" Sheriff Franklin asks.

He runs back into the building. The sheriff and Paul go after him. They find him upstairs.

"Put your hands up, Dr. Andrew," Sheriff Franklin yells.

Dr. Andrew slowly turns around with a small object in his right hand, saying, "I am here to carry out a mission directly from God. God has given me the power to purify mankind. The purification of mankind can be done only through the youth of man."

Detective White has his weapon pointed at Andrew and says, "Put the weapon down, Dr. Andrew, and put your hands up."

"I'm not afraid. I'm on a mission."

"For the last time, put the box down and raise your hands. If you don't, I will have to shoot you."

"I have a bomb in this box. All I have to do is activate it. You might not want to fire your weapon, Sheriff Franklin."

"You're giving me no choice." He fires and hits Dr. Andrew in his right shoulder, causing him to drop the box. The sheriff shoots him again in the leg, and he falls to the ground. Detective White goes over and kicks the box out of the way.

"Dr. Andrew, the God I know wouldn't want you to kill young boys to purify mankind," Sheriff Franklin says. "He would want you to mentor them and guide them down the right path."

"That's a bunch of hogwash. Nobody really took any interest in me when I was growing up. My father really isn't my father. My mother had an affair with my real father, and he didn't want me. I did what my mother expected of me."

"You can't choose your family."

Just then, the paramedics and police arrive to treat Dr. Andrew and get him to the hospital. Sheriff Franklin tells the police everything that's happened before he and Paul White head back to Marvell.

On the drive back, the sheriff says, "Paul, thank you for helping me solve these murders."

"You're welcome, Bob. It's had some twists and turns, and it's unfortunate that so many lives were cut short. I'm glad it's over. Well, it's back to New York for me. I think I'm going to stop in Chicago and get me a polish. I haven't had one in a while."

* * * *

Dr. Justice Andrew had trials in Baltimore, Memphis and Atlanta. Dr. Andrew had confessed to killings in Georgia after his arrest in Tennessee. Those boys' bodies were also found buried on his biological father's property in Arkansas.

A LOVER'S REVENGE

A DETECTIVE PAUL WHITE
MYSTERY #3

CHAPTER ONE

Romeo Martin, a 65-year-old retired medical examiner for the city of Houston, Texas, sits on his deck in Galveston, reminiscing about his past romantic relationships with different women over the last eight years. His one true love was his wife of 38 years, Rosemary Johnson. They got married right after their high school graduation. Since her death 10 years ago, he hasn't found anyone who moves him like Rosemary did. The women he has been involved with have ulterior motives. His children encouraged him to date, telling him their mother would want him to find happiness again. He found temporary happiness with the women, but it would start and stop rather suddenly. They lied to him and really didn't love him. Rosemary wasn't like that. She loved Romeo just the way he was. It didn't matter if he was poor or rich; as long as they were together, Rosemary was happy. If Rosemary was happy, he was happy.

He gets up from the chair and walks to the rail. The women he has dated made him do things he didn't want to do, but he couldn't control it. One day, he lost control and killed the first woman he had met after his wife's death. Wanda Mitchell had been very attractive, reminding him of Rosemary. In the end, all she saw was a widower whose wife had left him a lot of money. The day things came to a head, she said some cruel things to him and admitted to taking $5,000 from his checking account. That had put him over the edge, and he strangled her, putting all his rage into squeezing her neck. He felt a weight lift off him when he released her. Realizing now that he was gripping the rail, he lets go.

That was his cleanest kill. He's killed every single woman whom he's dated, eight in all. He became a different man after Rosemary died. He had never thought about killing a person or animal until after her death. *Why did you have to die and leave me here?* His experience as a medical examiner helped him make sure the murders couldn't be tied to him.

His thoughts turn to the second woman he killed, Janet Shepard. Along with reminding him of his wife, Janet had kept things hot in the bedroom like his wife had, but soon enough, things started to change.

Janet Shepard was a beautiful young, red-haired Irish girl with blue eyes, a rarity for a redhead. They met at the neighborhood grocery store where Janet worked as an assistant store manager. Romeo would visit twice a week just to see her and make small talk. Romeo became obsessed with her and started following her. When he followed her, he would create a situation where it seemed as if he had accidentally run into her.

One time she was having lunch with a girlfriend. Romeo was sitting at the bar having a drink. He decided to make his presence known and approached their table.

"Hello, Janet."

Janet had looked up, surprised to see Romeo. "Hello, Romeo. This is my friend, Martha. Martha, Romeo Martin."

"Pleasure to meet you, Martha."

"The same here, Romeo."

"I stopped in to get a bite to eat before going to my doctor's appointment, but when I saw you, I had to stop by and say hello. You are one of the most beautiful women I have seen in a long time."

Janet blushed, and Martha giggled.

"Will you ladies allow me to pay for your meal?"

"You don't have to do that, Romeo," Janet said.

"I want to. Please," he said.

"Okay, if you insist."

"I will take care of your bill and be on my way. It was a pleasure seeing you, Janet. Nice meeting you, Martha." He turned and walked away.

Soon after that encounter, Romeo and Janet began seeing each other regularly. Romeo wined and dined Janet, taking her on vacations to exotic locations in the Caribbean and Mexico. When they had reached their one-year anniversary, Romeo felt like he had found his perfect mate.

One summer evening, Janet had dinner with Martha. During their dinner, Martha said to Janet, "You seem to be really in love, girl, and Romeo is in love with you."

"I don't feel the same way about him. I appreciate all the gifts he's given me and the trips we've taken, but I don't love him."

"Why are you misleading him? You are going to break his heart. You need to break up with him before it's too late."

"If a man wants to buy me expensive things and take me on trips, that is on him. I'm only with him to make Jake jealous. Our relationship was fine until his mother started meddling."

"This is not going to end well, Janet. I'm telling you, you need to let Romeo go. It's not fair to him."

CHAPTER TWO

While Janet had been to dinner with Martha, Romeo had been trying to call Janet all day without any answer. Becoming worried, he decided to go to her apartment to check on her. Although Janet was not home, he saw an envelope taped to her door and notices it's from a man named Jake Duncan. *Who the hell is he?*

He pulled the envelope from the door and opened it. Inside was a single rose and a note saying, "I love you and miss you, Baby Girl. I need you. We need to get together soon."

Angry and confused, Romeo attached the envelope back to the door and left.

He thought to himself, *Baby Girl ... I love you ... Is Janet seeing another man?*

* * * *

A couple of days later, Romeo was out drinking with a couple of friends when he saw Janet having dinner with a man he didn't know. *Is that Jake?* Probably, he assumed, seeing the red roses on the table.

This is how she repays me? I'll show her, he thought. *She doesn't know who she's messing with.*

After one of his friends got his attention, he rejoined their conversation.

* * * *

After that, Janet and Jake revived their relationship, but she continued to see Romeo. She didn't know that Romeo had been following her. One Saturday afternoon, Janet and one of her girlfriends, Hilda Jennings, were shopping at the mall.

"Do you see that man standing over there in the brown jacket? Do you know him? I think that he is following us."

When Janet looked over at the man in the brown jacket, she answered, "I can't see his face."

Hilda said, "Let's start going in and out of different stores so we can determine whether that man is following us."

When Janet and Hilda come out of a dress store, Janet finally saw and recognized the man in the brown jacket.

"That's Romeo. Remember, I told you all about him. I'm beginning to have second thoughts about our relationship."

"Because of Jake?"

"Yes."

"You know what you need to do, but let's go say hello. I haven't met him in all this time."

They approached Romeo and when they were close enough, Janet said, "Romeo, what are you doing here?"

Romeo looked at her with a puzzled expression but recovered quickly. "Great minds must think alike. I'm just wasting a little time."

"It's been a while since I've seen you. Can we get together

soon? We really need to talk."

"What about now? I have some time."

"This really isn't the place for what I have to say."

"You're scaring me. How about we go over here where it's quiet and we can talk?"

"Okay," she said. She turned to Hilda. "I'll be back as soon as I can."

Romeo and Janet walked a short distance away and found a bench to sit on.

"What is it you have to say, Janet?"

"Romeo, I appreciate everything that you've given me and the time we've spent together, but you deserve someone who will make you happy."

"You make me happy, Janet."

"I'm not in love with you."

With that, Romeo jumped up and said angrily, "If that's the way you want it, fine!" He stormed off.

Hilda, who had seen Romeo leave, went over to her friend. "He looks real upset."

"I told him I'm not in love with him."

"Oh, man, but it's for the best."

"I know. My conscience was eating away at me. Let's get out of here."

* * * *

When Romeo walked back to his car, his thoughts centered on that punk, Jake. *After all that I have done for her, this is how she repays me? She's not going to get away with this.*

After getting into his car, he called his friend, Bill Evans, in Miami, who owns a nursery.

"Bill, did you order the plants I need?"

"Yes, they arrived today. I was getting them ready to be

sent to you. Are you sure you wanted hemlock and devil's helmet?"

"Yes, but there is no need to send them right now. I'll let you know when I need them."

Romeo knew that the devil's helmet is so toxic that a person has to wear gloves to handle it. If the plant is touched, it causes an arrhythmic heart function that leads to suffocation. Hemlock can kill as well. The person is paralyzed, and eventually, the respiratory system shuts down.

Romeo didn't see Janet for a while, but he spent the time plotting his revenge. All kinds of thoughts had run through his head, but he settled on his original plan to use the plants. When he had decided, he called Bill to have them delivered the next day. To cover his tracks, he made another call to make an airline reservation for the same day. He would stay away for about a month before returning to Galveston. By the time he returned, Janet would be dead. He had really liked her, but she deserved what he had planned for her.

A couple of weeks into his vacation, Romeo disconnected from a call with a friend of his back in Galveston. He had told him about the death of Janet Shepard. She and her friend, Hilda, had been out celebrating Hilda's birthday, drinking, eating and dancing the night away. The next day, Janet's boyfriend, Jake, found her dead on the bathroom floor. The cause of death was heart failure from an unknown substance in her system.

CHAPTER THREE

Jordan Williams has been a homicide detective for the Houston Police Department for the past 27 years, and he has three years before he retires. Detective Williams is presently in his office going through an old murder file. He's been temporarily assigned to look into eight cold cases. He's been investigating the open cases of several women, and from what he's gathered, he believes they may be connected. He's not sure how. All of the women died in a mysterious manner except for Wanda Mitchell, who was strangled with a person's bare hands.

There is little evidence in the files—no fingerprints, DNA, eyewitnesses or anything that could lead him to the possible killer. The cases of Janet Shepard, Beverly Rockford, Charlotte Winfield, Jennifer Romanati and Joan White have caught his attention. They all died of heart failure and had an unknown substance in their systems. The crime scene was too clean as if the person knew how to clean it. He currently examines the file of Beverly Rockford.

* * * *

Three months after Janet Shepard is found dead, Romeo is playing golf with one of his friends, Alex Murray. As they walk back into the club after playing the last hole, heading toward the country club dining room, Romeo suddenly looks over and sees a beautiful blonde woman with the body of a goddess. He turns and asks Alex, "Who is that fine lady standing over there?"

"I know her. That's Beverly Rockford. We went to high school together. She's divorced and has her own business as a CPA. I can introduce you to her if you want."

"That would be great!"

Alex and Romeo walk over to where Beverly is standing. Alex says, "Good evening, Beverly. How have you been doing?"

Beverly replies, "I'm just fine. How have things been going with you?"

"Things have been going well. Beverly, this is a friend of mine, Romeo Martin. Romeo, Beverly Rockford."

They both reply, "Pleasure to meet you."

Romeo says, "Beverly, would you like to join us for a bite to eat?"

"Sure."

After they take a seat and place their orders, they get into a lively discussion when Alex receives a call and excuses himself.

"Beverly, I hope you don't think this is too forward, but I think you are beautiful, and I would like to get to know you better. Would you be interested in getting to know me better?"

"I would."

"Here is my business card. Call me anytime."

Alex returns to the table and the conversation resumes.

* * * *

After many phone conversations between Beverly and Romeo, they agree to start dating. Romeo starts falling deeply in love with Beverly. He suddenly wants to be with Beverly all the time. Six months into their relationship, Beverly begins to feel that Romeo has become too aggressive, jealous and overbearing. Romeo starts following Beverly. When Beverly sees him parked in his car on her street as she's leaving for work, she decides she has had enough of Romeo. He has begun putting demands on her for her time and whereabouts. She divorced her second husband for this very reason. She needs some space.

A couple of days after the incident, Beverly tells Romeo over the phone that they are spending too much time together and she needs some space.

"Romeo, I really like you and enjoy spending time with you, but I think we need some time apart. I can't spend time with my friends and family because of your demands on my time."

"You don't like spending time with me, Beverly?"

Beverly sighs. "Romeo, I said I enjoy spending time with you, but because I am spending so much time with you, I no longer have time for myself. I need a break."

"You're seeing someone else, aren't you?"

"I'm not seeing someone else. I've told you this. The other day you showed up out of the blue at Leo's where I was having lunch with Pamela. I didn't even tell you that's where I was going. When I asked you about it, you said it was a coincidence. I'm beginning to believe there are no coincidences with you. This is why I need space. Goodbye, Romeo."

"But, Beverly ..." He hears the click of the phone.

The next day, he calls Beverly.

"Good evening, sweetheart. I know that you don't want to talk. I just want to apologize. I am truly sorry. I love you,

Beverly."

"I really care for you too. I need a break, Romeo. You're overbearing. Maybe it's best if we go our separate ways."

"Go our separate ways? Are you breaking up with me?"

"I wish you well, Romeo." She hangs up.

Romeo says to himself angrily, "How dare she break up with me? She's seeing someone, I know it. I will see her rot in hell before I see her with another man."

Six months later, Romeo is out and sees Beverly in a restaurant having dinner with another man. He becomes angry. *I knew she was seeing someone else. Telling me she wasn't seeing anyone. She must think I'm a fool. I'll show her who the fool is.*

Back at his apartment, Romeo starts plotting Beverly's murder. He looks at the poisonous plants with a smile. They worked quite well the last time. *Her time is coming.*

Romeo continues following Beverly, even breaking into her house and going through her things. He calls and hangs up frequently to scare her. One cool, summer night, Romeo is in a dark car with dark tinted windows parked directly across the street from Beverly's house. He sees Beverly come out of the house with a man and get into his car. *She's still seeing him.*

* * * *

He allows several weeks to go by before deciding to take a vacation to upstate New York. He covers his tracks well. All the right people know where he is vacationing. Three weeks into his vacation, a friend of his calls to tell him Beverly has been killed. Beverly was at a nightclub with one of her girlfriends celebrating her birthday. The next day Beverly was found dead in her car, leaning over the car steering wheel.

The cause of death is heart failure; an unknown substance was also found in her system.

Romeo says to himself, "I wonder who the next woman will be."

A week later, he returns to his life in Houston.

CHAPTER FOUR

Meanwhile, Detective Williams closes Beverly's file. There is something missing with these two cases. He wants to talk to her family members and friends in the hope that they can give him something new. He calls Janet's mother.

"May I speak with Theresa Shepard?"

"This is she. Who's calling?"

"Mrs. Shepard, I'm Detective Williams with the Houston Police Department."

"Did you find Janet's killer?"

"No, ma'am, not yet, but I am looking into your daughter's case."

"I want my daughter's killer found, Detective. It's been hard losing her."

"I understand, Mrs. Shepard. I have a couple of questions for you. Is this a good time?"

"Yes, it is. What would you like to ask me?"

"Was Janet dating anyone?"

"I'm not sure. We weren't very close, so I didn't know a lot about her personal life."

"I see," Detective Williams says. "As I've been reviewing her case, some things just aren't adding up."

"When I heard that she had died of heart failure, I knew something was wrong. We may not have been close, but I knew she didn't have any problems with her heart and she didn't do drugs."

"I plan on talking to her friend, Hilda. Do you know anyone else who I should talk to about Janet?"

"Hilda was her closest friend. They grew up together. If Janet had been dating anyone, Hilda would know."

"An interview wasn't done with her in the initial investigation. Do you know where I can contact Hilda?"

"I know she's a teacher at Garfield Elementary."

"Thank you, Mrs. Shepard. I'll update you with any new information."

"Thank you for looking into Janet's case. I know I can't bring my baby back, but I want someone to pay, Detective. Her life was stolen from her. She was too young to die."

"I can't make any promises, Mrs. Shepard, but I'll keep you informed."

He hangs up and calls Garfield Elementary to see if Hilda Jennings is at work. When he finds out she is there, he decides to go talk to her. He enters the school office and is greeted by a secretary.

"How may I help you?"

"I'm Detective Williams with the Houston Police Department, and I would like to speak with one of your teachers, Hilda Jennings, about a case I'm investigating."

"She's in class right now but will have a break soon. If you don't mind waiting, I'll let her know."

"I can wait."

The bell rings, and a few minutes later, Hilda walks into the office.

"Hilda, Detective Williams is right there."

"Detective, what can I do for you?"

"Is there someplace private we can talk?"

"We can go to my room. I have my planning period now."

They leave the office and go to her room on the second floor.

"Ms. Jennings, I'm investigating Janet Shepard's case."

"Have you found something new?"

"No, that's why I'm here."

"How can I help?"

"At the time of Janet's death, was she seeing anyone else besides Jake Duncan?"

"At the time of her death, she had recently stopped seeing an older gentleman named Romeo. She never told me his last name. All I know is he was retired and lived in Galveston. I was there the day she broke up with him. He had become possessive, and she wanted to get back with Jake."

"Is there anything else you remember?"

"She told me he plays golf at the country club by the grocery store where she worked. The name of the country club is Sutton Hills."

"You've given me some helpful information, Ms. Jennings. Thank you."

"Janet has been gone two years, and I miss her. She didn't deserve to die. If there is anything else I can help you with, please let me know."

"Let me leave you with my card so you can contact me in case you remember anything else."

"Thank you."

Detective Williams leaves the school. When he gets back to his office, he starts the process for getting a search warrant to get a membership list from the country club. After hanging up the phone, he goes to inform his boss, Chief of Detectives Bobby Jones, about the new information in the case of Janet Shepard. He knocks on the door and waits to be invited inside.

"Come in," Detective Jones says as he looks up and lays down his pen. "Jordan, anything new in those cases?"

"Actually, yes. I spoke to a friend of Janet Shepard, and she gave me information about a man Janet was seeing before she was killed. She didn't have his last name, but she knew his first name and the country club where he played golf. I've requested a search warrant for the membership list of the Sutton Country Club."

"They aren't going to like giving their membership list to us," Jones says. "The thought of one of their members being a killer is a scandal they don't want."

"I know. These cases are still stumping me, Chief."

"You're looking at eight cases, right?"

"Yes, sir."

"I don't have any more manpower I can spare right now. I do know someone I can call who can assist you with the investigation."

"You do?"

"Yes, Paul White. He's a retired detective from Chicago. He was my partner when I worked for the Chicago P.D. Let me give him a call and see if he can come down to help. I'll let you know if he's available."

Detective Jones dials his friend's number after Detective Williams leaves his office.

"Hello, Paul?"

"Yes, this is Paul."

"This is Bobby Jones."

"Bobby! How are you?"

"I'm doing well."

"Good. How is Marion doing?"

"She's doing much better now that she's in remission."

"Wonderful news! I'm so excited to hear she's in remission. I'll continue to pray for her and you. I know it hasn't been easy for you."

"No, it hasn't, but your counsel has helped me tremendously. Listening to you share your experience about when your wife had cancer helped me get through this."

"I'm glad, Bobby."

"Me too. But that's not why I called. One of my detectives is looking into eight cold cases. The women were all killed, and he's looking for a connection. He might be close, but he needs another pair of eyes."

Paul chuckles. "When do you need me?"

"How soon can you get here?"

"I'm in Fort Worth visiting my grandson, who's a freshman at Texas Christian University. I was planning on heading back home tomorrow, but I can swing down your way instead."

Bobby laughs. "Great! You'll be working with Detective Jordan Williams. He's a good detective."

"Okay. I'll see you tomorrow."

CHAPTER FIVE

Romeo hangs up from talking to his friend, Marshall Winfield, who informed him he's getting married again. *I told him he would be better off without that wife of his.*

Yes, the memory was painful. A year after Beverly's death, he was playing golf with Marshall.

* * * *

"Tell me, Marshall, what's been going on in your life? You seem distracted."

"Man, my damn wife left me and took the kids with her."

"Did Charlotte catch you with another woman?"

"Hell no, man! I never cheated on my wife. I think she's having an affair with someone she works with. I love that woman more than life itself. How in the world can she justify taking my kids and leaving me for another man? I have worked and sacrificed my ass off to give her and the children the best, and this is how she treats me."

"I wish that I could tell you what do, but whatever you decide, I've got your back."

"I have no idea what I'm going to do."

"Fight for your kids. I'll be a character witness if you need me."

"Thanks, Romeo. I'll let you know what I decide."

After Romeo and Marshall finish their last hole of golf, they both leave the country club for home. A week later, Romeo is out one evening at a local bar having some drinks and trying to relax. He looks over and sees Marshall's wife, Charlotte, sitting at a table with another man. Romeo stops one of the waitresses and asks her, as he points a finger toward Charlotte's table, "Do you see the woman over there sitting with the man at that table? Do you know who she is?"

The waitress replies, "Yes, she's here all the time. She's been a working girl for some time. Would you like to meet her? I can introduce you to her, if that is what you're looking for."

"That's okay. She just looked familiar to me."

The waitress walks off, and Romeo soon leaves. On the way to his car, he thinks, *I hope Marshall and the kids never find out she's a hooker.*

The following week, Marshall calls Romeo to tell him that his wife has filed for a divorce and has taken $10,000 from his personal savings account.

"Charlotte is really trying to mess me over. She's trying to take everything that I worked hard to earn. I'm so mad I could kill her."

"You don't really want to do that, Marshall."

"I know, I know. I just can't believe it."

Romeo sees Charlotte out more often, and Marshall keeps calling him to complain about one thing or another that she has done. *I might have to take care of this situation myself.*

One night, Romeo is in a bar having a drink when he sees Charlotte with another man. Charlotte stands up and walks toward his table.

"I am so tired of you being all up in my personal business! You are just like my weak ass husband. The both of you can go straight to hell! As for your friend, he's going to wish he never married me."

Romeo rises from his table smiling and says, "I'm sure we'll see you in hell." He walks out of the bar. *Her time is up.*

A few days before Thanksgiving, Romeo is talking to Marshall. "I'm going be out of town for a while."

"Where are you going?"

"Upstate New York. I'll be there until New Year's Eve."

"Enjoy yourself. Wish I could come with you, but Charlotte is letting the kids come over for Thanksgiving."

"Good. Enjoy the time with your kids, and I'll check in with you while I'm away."

One rainy night, Charlotte is at a local hotel having sex with one of her johns. On her way home, she suddenly feels pains in her chest and passes out while she is driving, hitting an oncoming bus. The medical examiner's report says that Charlotte's death was from heart failure, possibly from an unknown drug. Marshall, with the deepest sorrow in his voice, calls Romeo to tell him about Charlotte's death.

As Romeo looks out the window of his hotel, he thinks to himself, *Marshall, my friend, Charlotte was no good, and I did you a favor getting rid of her. She didn't deserve you.*

* * * *

Detective Paul White is with Detective Williams in Chief Jones's office.

"Paul, thank you again for coming to help Jordan with the cases. Jordan, please update Paul on the cases."

"I'm focusing on the case of Janet Shepard. She was found

dead by her boyfriend in the bathroom. The cause of death was heart failure, and she had an unknown substance in her system. Seven of the women had the same cause of death. I spoke to Ms. Shepard's friend yesterday, and she gave me the first name of a man Janet had dated previously and the country club where he is a member. I got a search warrant for the membership list and received the list this morning. I found someone who is a member with the first name I was given, Romeo Martin."

"Paul, you must be good luck because Jordan didn't have a lead before today."

Paul and Bobby laugh as Detective Williams continues. "Romeo Martin is a retired medical examiner with homes in Houston and Galveston."

"We need to get in contact with him as soon as possible," Chief Jones says.

"I was planning on contacting him today."

"Great. What else do you have?

"The killings of the eight women have to be connected because I don't think it's a coincidence they all died the same way," Detective White says.

"I think you're correct, Paul," Detective Williams says.

"Let me take a look at the files while you call Romeo Martin, Jordan."

"I'll let you two get on with the case. Keep me updated."

Jordan and Paul leave the office. Jordan sets Paul up at a desk so he can begin going over the files, and Jordan goes to his office to call Romeo Martin.

"Hello."

"Yes. I'm trying to reach Romeo Martin."

"This is him. Who's calling?"

"I'm Detective Williams with the Houston Police Department. I'm investigating a case, and your name came up as a person I should contact."

The hairs on the back of his neck stand up. "What kind of investigation?"

"The murder of Janet Shepard."

Silence.

"Mr. Martin, are you still there?"

"Yes, yes I am. I don't know a Janet Shepard, so I don't know why my name would come up in your investigation."

"I was given your name by someone who said she dated you prior to her death."

"No, the name isn't ringing a bell."

"Are you sure?"

Romeo replies angrily, "Look, Detective, I told you I don't know a Janet Shepard! Don't call me again!"

He disconnects the call and begins pacing and saying, "Who gave him my name? It must be one of Janet's friends. Ugh! I can't remember their names. It will come to me. I just have to calm down and think. It will come to me."

As he takes a seat on the couch, he thinks about one of the women he's killed. That always seems to soothe him. His fourth victim comes to mind, Jennifer Romanati. She was a beautiful Italian woman with an hourglass figure. He first saw her when he was out celebrating his 59th birthday.

He was at the bar getting a drink when he noticed the woman in a red silk dress. He asked the bartender if he knew her, and when he said he didn't, he offered to ask the waitresses for Romeo.

Romeo went to the restroom, and when he returned, he asked the bartender, "What happened to the lady in the red dress?"

"I think she left. I did hear her tell her friend that she would be having her birthday celebration here a week from today."

"Thanks," Romeo said before going back to his own celebration.

The next week, Romeo went back to the bar and found the lady in the red dress was there as planned. This time she was wearing a red wrap dress. He approached her to introduce himself. They hit it off and ended up dancing the night away. They talked on the phone and went on dates to get to know each other better. Soon their relationship intensified. They spent many hours making love. Their time together reminded Romeo of the passion he and his wife, Rosemary, had shared. As the months went by, Romeo began to keep tabs on Jennifer by following her. She got tired of it and ended their relationship. He continued to follow her and discovered when she began dating someone else.

He planned another vacation to New York. While out of town, he learned about her death. Her new boyfriend had found her dead body in the bedroom. The cause of death was respiratory failure, more than likely caused by an unknown substance in her system.

CHAPTER SIX

Detective White closes Jennifer Romanati's file as Detective Williams walks up to the desk.

"I just got off the phone with Romeo Martin."

"What were you able to find out?"

"He said he doesn't know a Janet Shepard, but I think he does. He got quite angry at the end of our call and hung up on me. He's hiding something."

"Looks like we need to focus on Romeo Martin," Detective White says.

"I agree. Maybe we'll have some luck at the country club. Let's go."

At the country club, the detectives do not find a lot of people who are willing to talk. The people who do answer their questions state that they have seen him at the club on several occasions, but nothing else. As they head out to Detective Williams's car, they meet one of the valets.

Detective Williams says, "Excuse me, sir, I'm a detective for the Houston Police Department, and this is my associate, Detective White. We are investigating a case and wanted to know if we could ask you a few questions."

"Sure. I've worked here for over 30 years. I know pretty much everything that goes on here."

"What's your name?"

"Robert Shelton."

"Mr. Shelton, do you know a member named Romeo Martin?"

"Yes, I do. I've seen him on several occasions. What about him?"

"He's a person of interest in one of my cases. What can you tell me about him?"

"He's been quite the lady's man since his wife died 10 years ago. He's like a Dr. Jekyll and Mr. Hyde. I see him here at the club and at Houston Executive Airport where I have a part-time job."

"Does he travel a lot?"

"Several times a year. I don't know why his cousin lets him fly his plane. I always wondered if he was hiding something. Both of them are off their rocker."

"When did you last see him?"

"It's been a while … maybe a month ago here at the club. He was with a young lady. He likes them young and shapely."

"Thank you, Mr. Shelton. You've been quite helpful."

"I hope he hasn't done anything too bad, but I wouldn't put it past him. You all take care."

The detectives return to headquarters and head straight to Chief Jones's office to update him.

"I've got to request another search warrant to take a look at the security cameras at the country club. I'm going to need someone to go through them."

"Okay. Let me know when you get the disc, and I'll pull someone to look through it for you," Chief Jones says.

* * * *

A couple of days later, Detective White and Williams are discussing the case.

"Jordan, I found something in the file of Catherine Maddox. The substance found in her body included hemlock and devil's helmet."

"I haven't had a chance to review her file yet. That's useful information."

"Yes, it is. I feel we need to have that substance tested again on the other women. We need to have it sent to a lab. I have a feeling the results are going to be the same."

"I'll take care of it. I just got off the phone with the officer who was looking at the security camera footage, and he's found Romeo Martin on the tape with a woman like Mr. Shelton described. We got an anonymous tip saying that Romeo Martin has been going to New York every year for the last eight years using a private jet."

"I wonder when those trips took place."

"I'd have to get a search warrant for the flight records. I don't want to get ahead of myself, but I'm beginning to think Romeo Martin is our guy."

"Me too."

Detective Williams orders the tests to look for hemlock or devil's helmet in the other victims and starts the process for obtaining a search warrant for the flight records. Paul researches the plants and discovers that they are poisonous—so poisonous, in fact, that you should wear gloves when handling them.

* * * *

Romeo is out with his friends, Alex and Marshall, having dinner when he spots his most recent love interest, Vickie Gibson. She is with two men he doesn't recognize.

"Excuse me for a minute. I'll be right back."

He gets up and approaches Vickie's table.

"Are you two-timing me, Vickie?"

Vickie turns in shock to see Romeo standing behind her.

"I told you that I don't want to talk to you. Now, please leave."

"I'm not going anywhere until I find out who these fools are with my woman."

"I am not your woman any longer, Romeo! I wish you would leave me alone. For your information, this is my brother, Andy, and my minister, Reverend Jackson. We were discussing my grandmother's funeral arrangements ... the grandmother you didn't believe I was going to see in South Carolina who was dying. Just go away."

Romeo goes back to his table and Vickie's brother says, "Vic, I'm going to stay a little longer. I don't trust that old dude. I can take the time off."

When Romeo returns to his friends' table, he excuses himself and goes home. On the drive home, he recalls when he first met Vickie.

* * * *

He noticed her working in Harris's Barbershop and Salon in the mall. Three weeks later, he sees Vickie at the country club having dinner with a group of people at the table next to where he was just seated. He makes small talk with the group.

"Forgive me, ladies. I haven't introduced myself. My name is Romeo."

The ladies introduce themselves as Vickie, Shirley, Rose and Stephanie. They continue their dinner, and when Romeo notices Vickie getting up, he follows her. When she comes out of the bathroom, he's waiting for her.

"Romeo, you startled me."

'I apologize. I didn't mean to. I just wanted to talk to you in private for a moment. I would really like to get to know you better. Can I take you out some time?"

"I'm not sure right now. Maybe I can call you?"

"Sure, sure. Here's my card. I hope to hear from you soon."

Romeo leaves the club, and Vickie returns to her dinner companions. Two weeks pass without Romeo hearing from Vickie. *Maybe she's been busy,* he tells himself. He decides to go out for a drink. After he's been at the bar a while, he notices Vickie is there with a group of ladies shooting pool. He's a little tipsy, but he goes over to say hello.

"Vickie, I thought I would have heard from you by now."

"Oh, hi, Romeo! I've been meaning to call, but I had to go to South Carolina to see my grandmother who is in a nursing home. I just got back, and my girlfriends wanted to take me out to lift my spirits."

"I hope your grandmother is doing okay. I just wanted to say hello. Give me a call when you get a chance."

He walks off. Romeo and Vickie begin seeing each other, and just like all his other relationships, he begins to distrust her. He follows her everywhere she goes. Yet Vickie doesn't break things off with Romeo until she tells him that she has to go to see her grandmother again in South Carolina.

"Romeo, I told you. My grandmother isn't doing well, and I need to see her because she is dying."

"You're going off with some man, I know it!"

"I am not! I wish you would get it through your head that I am not cheating on you," she says. "Romeo, you have changed since we first started seeing each other, and I don't like it. You don't trust me; you're always accusing me of cheating. I can't be in a relationship with someone who doesn't trust me."

"But, I love you, Vickie."

"I don't need that kind of love. I need to concentrate on my grandmother. Goodbye, Romeo. Don't contact me anymore."

She's just like the rest. Her time is coming.

CHAPTER SEVEN

Detective Williams receives the break he has been needing. The flight records show that Romeo Martin was always in upstate New York at the time of the murders.

"Paul, Romeo Martin has a trip to New York planned soon."

"When?"

"In a week."

"We don't have much time. We need to find out who he's been seeing recently. Have you heard back from the country club?"

Before Williams can answer, his phone rings.

"Williams."

"Detective, this is Mr. Shelton from the country club. The officer you sent is here. I just looked at the picture, and I know the young lady. Her name is Vickie Gibson; she works at Harris's Barbershop and Salon. I get my haircut there every week."

"Thank you, Mr. Shelton. You have been a big help," Detective Williams says. "Paul, let's go. Mr. Shelton just ID'd the woman in the video as Vickie Gibson, and she works at a local barbershop."

When they arrive at the salon, they ask the receptionist for Vickie.

"I'm Vickie."

"Ms. Gibson, I'm Detective Williams, and I have reason to believe your life is in danger. Do you know Romeo Martin?"

"My life is in danger? Yes, I know Romeo. I recently broke up with him."

"He is a person of interest in several murder cases. We think you might be his next victim. We'll need you to come with us."

The detectives leave with Vickie to take her home to pick up a few belongings. Unbeknownst to the detectives and Vicki, Romeo has broken into Vickie's house. After walking around, he sets out to do what he's come to do. *Too bad, I really liked her.*

Vickie and the detectives walk into the kitchen in time to see Romeo pouring something into the orange juice.

"Freeze, Romeo," Detective Williams yells as he reaches for his weapon. "Put the items on the counter and raise your hands."

Romeo slowly complies, and Detective Williams rushes over to cuff him, then he calls for backup.

On their way to the station, Detective White says, "Jordan, you've done a great job with these cases. You really didn't need my help."

"Paul, you were very helpful. I really appreciate you coming to help."

"No problem. Retirement isn't all it's cracked up to be. I need something to keep me busy every now and then. Working these cases helps keep an old man sane."

* * * *

Three months later, Detective Williams is talking to Chief Jones.

"Good work, Jordan, solving those cases."

"I didn't do it by myself. Paul was gracious enough to stay on for a month while I finished the investigation."

"I can't believe Romeo Martin didn't commit those murders."

"That's because the person I arrested three months ago wasn't really Romeo Martin. The real Romeo Martin has been dead for over 10 years. Romeo's twin brother, Diablo Martin, took on his identity after escaping a mental facility. Diablo is bipolar with symptoms of schizophrenia. He believes he *is* his brother."

"Didn't Romeo's wife die eight years ago?"

"Yes, at the hands of Diablo when she found out his true identity. He had been pretending to be Romeo for two years before she figured it out. I'm glad the families have closure now."

CONVICTION
OF AN INNOCENT
MAN

A DETECTIVE PAUL WHITE
MYSTERY #4

CHAPTER ONE

Carnell Johnson has been in the Georgia State Prison in Reidsville for 10 years serving a life sentence for the murder of three of his closest friends. He was 29 when he was sentenced. Carnell grew up in one of the largest and poorest neighborhoods in southeastern Atlanta, Lakewood Heights. The oldest of 10 children, he was raised by his mother because his father left the family one night shortly after their fifth child was born. He told them he found a better paying job in Chicago, but he couldn't bring the family with him right away. He would let them know when they could join him. Carnell and his family never heard from him again. His mother was left to raise the five children alone. She tried her best, but her choices in men were questionable, and each resulted in a pregnancy. None of them stuck around because they didn't want the burden of raising someone else's children. Carnell stepped up to provide for his family by committing petty crimes and hustling on the streets of Atlanta, working his way up to being a drug dealer.

When he was 12, he was arrested for the first time for

possession, and he has been in and out of jail since that time for various crimes. His mother was murdered when he was 16 as they were coming out of a grocery store. She died in his arms. At that time, the ages of his siblings ranged from 6 to 15. The younger six children were sent to various family members. Carnell raised his brother and twin sisters, who were one and two years younger than him, respectively. He knew his mother had hated the life he led and didn't want her other children to go down the same path. Neither did he. However, three of his siblings did follow him into the game. The rest were able to make better lives for themselves.

Living as an inmate has been cruel and dangerous for Carnell. There have been three attempts on his life. He's been purposely committing serious prison violations so he would be put in solitary confinement because he feared for his life. Someone wants him dead.

One afternoon, Carnell gets a chance to talk to his childhood friend, James Richardson, who is in jail for possession of marijuana. James has been at the prison for six months and recently got reacquainted with Carnell when he began working in the laundry room. They used to run the streets together when they were 10 years old. They lost touch when James and his family moved from Atlanta when he was 12.

"Hey, my brother, I know that you didn't murder those guys. They were like family to you. You had to be set up by someone."

Carnell replies, "James, man, I know. I'm not a saint, but I want to know who wants me dead."

"Getting out of here might be your only option or else you are going to end up dead way before your time."

"Keep it down. You don't know who might be listening," Carnell says as he looks around. "I don't know the first thing about trying to get out of here."

"Me either, but I know it's been done. I can at least see what I can find out about who wants you dead."

"Okay," Carnell says. "I'll do the same."

"Hey, you two, stop talking and get back to work," a correction officer tells Carnell and James.

***

At the Federal Bureau of Investigation in Washington, D.C., Randall Morris, the agent in charge of the investigation into the Manuel drug cartel, which operates in the Southeast region of the United States, is talking to fellow agent David Woody about information he has recently received from his team working the case.

"David, I just reviewed this report about the Manuel drug cartel. There are some pictures in it I want to show you."

Agent Morris slides the pictures over to Agent Woody to review.

"See anyone who catches your eye?" Agent Morris asks.

Agent Woody leans up in his chair to get a better look and says, "Is that Michael Vecchio? The other guy looks like Vince Vecchio, his cousin. Who are the other guys in the picture?"

"Yes, they are from the Vecchio family, and they are meeting with Edward Morgan and Justin Cooper, high-ranking members of the Manuel cartel."

"Is Michael Vecchio trying to spread his wings? His grandfather isn't going to be happy when he finds out Michael is doing business with a drug cartel."

"That's why I brought this to you. What do you know about the Vecchio family?"

"The family is from Sicily and is led by "Papa" John Vecchio out of New York. They are not into drugs or prostitution. It's even in their family creed. They hide their money in their trucking and food service businesses, and they are one of the last Mafia families to still have a casino in Las Vegas."

"My guys believe Michael is trying to make a move in the family."

"John Vecchio is old school and believes in the traditional ways. Michael is up to something because the Vecchio family doesn't operate in the South. What do you want to do?"

"I've got a few agents inside, but one of them almost blew the case, so I'm going to have to pull him off. He was Michael's driver and was able to find out a lot of information. My agents are telling me he's starting to get too comfortable and has let a few things slip. But they don't think Michael suspects anything yet."

"I know someone we can bring in to take his place whom you can trust."

"You do?"

"Yes, my friend Paul White. He's a retired Chicago police detective who helped me out with a case in Arkansas. He can be trusted. I can call him right now and see if he's available."

"If you trust him, call him. I don't want this case to blow up and have the DEA turn us into a laughingstock."

Agent Woody makes the call to his friend. "Paul, David Woody here."

"David, it's been a while. How are you?"

"I'm doing well. I hope I didn't catch you at a bad time because I was calling for another favor."

"What do you need me to do?"

"I need you to go undercover in Atlanta as a driver for Michael Vecchio, who is being investigated."

"You caught me at a good time. When do I need to be there?"

The agents go on to explain everything about the case to Paul and make arrangements for him to fly from his home in New York to Atlanta the next day.

***

At the Georgia State Prison, Carnell and James are finished with the laundry and are going through the end-of-day process before being cleared to return to their cells. The correction officers are checking them to make sure they aren't smuggling anything back to the cell blocks. After they are cleared, Carnell wonders where the guy behind him came from because he isn't from his cell block. Before he can say anything, the guy stabs him repeatedly with a shank. A few minutes pass before the officers restrain the inmate stabbing Carnell. Because of his injuries, Carnell is sent to the emergency room at a nearby hospital.

CHAPTER TWO

While Carnell is recovering from the vicious stabbing, an FBI agent from the regional office in Atlanta places a call to Warden Jackson Smiley at the Georgia State Prison.

"Warden Smiley, it seems like you don't have things under control at your prison."

"Agent Carter, things are in control."

"You're delusional. Carnell Johnson was stabbed yesterday, and your correctional officers let it happen. I told you I need him to stay alive because he is key to the case I'm working."

"How did you find out about that?"

"Corruption is running rampant in your prison, Warden."

"I have two of my officers with him 24/7, and when he is allowed to return, he will be moved to isolation permanently."

"Not good enough. I don't trust your people, Jackson. Here's what's going to happen. Two of my agents are arriving at the hospital in the next hour where Carnell is recuperating. You are to meet them there and proceed to his room to relieve your officers. My agents will stay with him until he is cleared to be released. Once he is cleared for release, he will be sent to a safe house near Atlanta where I can keep an eye on him."

"Ronald, it doesn't have to come to this."

"Yes, it does. This is the fourth time someone has tried to kill him!"

"Look, I got rid of the officers who let that last attack happen."

"Too little, too late. We do it my way. I will send you the information you need to make his transfer legit, and I am having you removed from that position."

"My job, Ronald?!"

"Cuz, I got your back. You've served your purpose there. You'll be with Carnell at the safe house as a guard. He's never seen you, right?"

"Right."

"No problem. You better get moving," Agent Carter says and hangs up. Warden Smiley gets his jacket and heads to the hospital.

***

Michael and Vince Vecchio are in the car on their way to a meeting with members of the Manuel cartel when Michael begins a conversation with the driver. "Sam highly recommended you, Mr. White."

"Paul. Please, call me Paul," Detective White says.

"Paul, how did you all know each other?"

"We served a short time in jail together and have been friends ever since."

"That's what he told me. Thank you for stepping in for him while he deals with a family emergency."

"It was no problem. His mother is like a mother to me, and I was saddened to hear about her failing health. I was glad to help him out."

"A measure of a true friend. Paul, you may see and hear some things that I expect you to keep to yourself."

"Of course."

Detective White pulls the car to a stop a few feet away from another vehicle in an underground parking garage. Michael and Vince get out and greet Edward Morgan and Justin Cooper of the Manuel cartel.

Edward says, "Good morning Michael, Vince. Before we get down to business, I just want to say we are looking forward to working with y'all. The doors you've opened for us are already paying off."

"I have big plans for all of us in the next few months that will make us rich," says Michael. "Were you able to make contact with the seller?"

"Yes. The deal is set for next week at the usual place at 8."

"And ... you trust him?"

"Yes, he knows the score."

"Okay. I'll check with you in a few days."

***

At a hospital somewhere in Georgia, inmate Carnell Johnson is recovering from the most recent attack on his life. He summons one of the agents to his bedside.

"Where are the guards who were here?"

"The warden relieved them of their duty and personally hired our security firm to guard you while you recover."

"It's about time he started stepping up. A lot of those COs in that prison are dirty. I hope you all can do a better job."

"We've not lost a client yet."

***

A couple of weeks later, Carnell receives an unexpected guest, James Richardson. Carnell smiles when he sees James, bruised, bandaged and in a hospital robe, enter his room.

"Man, I thought that asshole killed you. I was praying you would make it."

"Yeah, me too. Have you been hospitalized this whole time?"

"No, I was here for a couple of days. There were two guys—one attacked you and the other attacked me," James says to Carnell. "I learned they work for whoever wants you dead."

"Damn!"

"That place is so crooked. You can't go back, Carnell."

"What do you expect me to do? It's not like I can just walk out of here. How did you get back here?"

"I guess I asked the wrong person some questions and got attacked again. I know I'm onto something, but we need to get out of here. Let me think on it; I'll be back."

"James, you know I never thought you would end up in jail, let alone prison, but I'm glad you're here. I know you have my back."

"Things change, and you never know where life will take you. Don't worry, Carnell, I got you."

***

Papa John Vecchio is sitting at a table in his wine cellar, meeting with the family lawyer, Terry Madison; the underboss, Carlo Fabbri; and John's consigliere, Tom Palma, his right-hand man.

"Papa John, I just learned the Feds are investigating the Vecchio family for prostitution and drug trafficking," the lawyer says.

"What?! We aren't involved in those types of things," John Vecchio says.

"I know, sir. That's what I was told. Plus, three of our men were killed in Atlanta."

"What were they doing in Atlanta, James?"

"I'm not quite sure."

"Since the days of our existence, it has been our creed and honor to stay out of prostitution and the drug business. The Vecchio family does not disrespect women, and our only vice is alcohol. We don't need the Feds meddling in our business. There must be a traitor. We need to find out who it is and take care of them as soon as possible."

"Don, let me make some inquiries," Tom says.

"Okay. Whoever he is, the traitor will pay with his life."

CHAPTER THREE

Agent Morris phones Detective White. "Have you been able to find out anything?"

"The grandson, Michael, is definitely working a deal with the cartel. His cousin is just along for the ride. There was a deal that was supposed to go down, but it's been called off. Three of Michael's men were killed. He's not sure who killed them. I'm thinking it's the cartel or someone else who doesn't want Michael in their territory," reports Paul.

"His grandfather doesn't know what he's up to, so Michael can't ask him for help. He's on his own, which is good because he's bound to mess up sooner or later. I'll have one of my agents look into the murders. Let me know when the deal is back on," Agent Morris says.

***

It's been a week since James visited Carnell at the undisclosed hospital, and mysteriously, he's back with a plan.

"Carnell, we're getting out of here today. An inmate from

the prison is here who just died during surgery. He looks like you. I found a way to switch you with him."

"How are you going to do that?"

"Someone will take you to X-ray, and that is where we will do the switch. This person can be trusted, so don't worry. We will be gone by the time they bring the dead prisoner back to your room."

"James, you are the only person I trust. If you say I can trust them, I will. I just hope this works."

"It will."

James leaves the room, and about 15 minutes later, a transporter arrives to take Carnell to get an X-ray. The guard stops him before he enters the room.

"What are you doing here?"

"I'm here to take Carnell Johnson to get an X-ray," he says, showing the guard the paperwork.

"Okay, go on, but one of us is coming with you."

"No problem."

The transporter, Carnell and the guard leave the room and head to the elevators leading to Radiology. When the elevator arrives, Carnell is moved in, then the guard. The transporter moves up behind the guard as the doors close and strikes him at the base of his skull, knocking the guard out. Carnell is in awe as he sees this happen.

"Damn!"

As the doors open again, James is waiting for him.

"Nice work," James says as he grabs Carnell's bed and heads in the opposite direction of Radiology, onto another elevator then out of the hospital.

***

Some time later, the guard wakes up, finds himself still in the elevator and tries to stand. After stumbling a little, he is able to get back on his feet. He looks over to the transport bed and notices right away the person in the bed is not Carnell.

"Shit!"

He frantically tries to get the elevator moving. After pushing several buttons, it begins to move and the doors open to the floor where Carnell was being held. As soon as the doors open, he exits, rushing to the room.

"Sir, Carnell Johnson has escaped."

"Escaped! What do you mean he escaped?"

"We were on the elevator, and the next thing I knew, I was on the ground. I must've been hit from behind and passed out. When I woke up, there was a dead man on the elevator, but it wasn't Carnell."

"Unbelievable," the agent says as he shakes his head and begins pacing. "Unbelievable. You lost him on your watch, so you have to call."

"Sir, I think ..."

"I don't care what you think. Make the damn call and explain to the warden how you lost his prisoner."

As the other guard makes the call, he turns toward the window and sees a black vehicle speeding away from the hospital.

***

Agent Morris has just been informed that Carnell Johnson has escaped from the facility where he was being held by the warden.

"Jackson, you said you had this under control."

"I did. You know those guys I had guarding Carnell are great at their jobs. They've worked for you before. Someone else had a hand in this. Probably James Richardson."

"Who is James Richardson?"

"You know who he is. He had your permission to visit Carnell."

"I don't know a James Richardson, and I didn't give anybody permission to visit him."

"Well, he knows you because the guards said they received the okay from their boss. He's visited him twice."

"Jackson, did anybody think to check with me?"

"Hey, I just found out about this myself, so don't blame me."

"There is someone else who has a vested interest in Carnell Johnson. I need to find out who and find them and this James Richardson. Send me all the information you have on Richardson while he was in prison," he says, hanging up abruptly.

Why would anyone go through all the trouble to help him escape? I'm missing something.

After going through the information the warden sent him about James Richardson, Agent Morris makes a call to Detective White. "Detective, can you talk?"

"Yes."

"There is a prisoner at the Georgia State Prison, Carnell Johnson, who has had several attempts on his life. Somehow, he is connected to either the Manuel cartel or Michael Vecchio. I need you to keep an eye out for him or James Richardson. I'll send you their pictures. They recently escaped."

"Okay. That deal is back on, by the way. I'll let you know when I find out the details."

"Great," he says and hangs up. Agent Morris also informs his undercover agent in the Manuel cartel as well as the other agents on the case about the escaped prisoners.

***

Somewhere in an abandoned building outside the city of Atlanta, Carnell and James are trying to get some rest before they begin their search to find out who put a hit on Carnell.

James says, "I know you're in a great deal of pain, but we're going to have to move soon. I spread the word that I was out of prison, and my guys are on their way. They can protect us. Can you think of any reason why your three friends were killed? Did you have a drug deal gone wrong?"

"I can't think of anything."

"Why were you left alive? Someone wants you to take the fall."

"Now that I think more on it, the only time we came in contact with any significant dealers was the time we helped guard the private party at The Thyme. There were some major drug players there, but we were just there as security."

James says, "Maybe there was someone there who you and your boys were not supposed to see. If so, we have to find out who that person was and then we can learn who wants you dead."

CHAPTER FOUR

At The Thyme in the wine cellar, the Vecchios, their driver Paul, Edward Morgan and Justin Cooper are meeting.

Edward addresses the Vecchios. "Michael, Vince, who is this?"

"This is Paul, our new driver and guard. He's cool," Michael replies.

"Okay. Thanks for meeting with us on such short notice. We have some concerns about our deal. We may have to delay it."

"Delay it, for what reason?"

"We're concerned about getting involved with your family, Michael. You told me yourself this is a new venture for you. Are you sure everyone is on board?"

Michael replies, "Gentlemen, you have nothing to worry about. I already have everything in place for you to make your move to the East Coast. As far as the leadership in my family, there is about to be a big change. My grandfather is retiring, and we are looking to move in a different direction. I have already put things in motion. I can assure you, there will not be a problem. I am a man of my word. Now, let's get down to business."

Unbeknownst to everyone else, Detective White is wired, and the meeting is being listened to by FBI agents Vincent Malone and Brad Guarino.

***

Carnell and James got into the black vehicle outside of the abandoned building where they were hiding. James' men inform them that the authorities are looking for them.

James says, "It's a good thing I thought about getting us new disguises. Jessie does good work. You won't know it's you after she's done."

"James, man, I can't thank you enough for what you're doing."

"No problem, Carnell. It's all good."

The car heads to a location where Jessie Mercy, the makeup artist, is waiting for them. After several hours, the men emerge with new looks and clothes.

"James, you were right! Your girl is on point. I look like a totally different person."

"I told you she was good. Now, let's get this show on the road and find out what's going on in the ATL."

***

In New York, Papa John Vecchio is meeting with three members of the family council, including Carlo Fabbri and Tom Palma, to discuss the traitor in the family.

"Don, the people I sent to Atlanta have found out the identity of the traitor in the family."

Papa John sits up straight in his chair as he asks, "Who is it?"

"Michael and Vince."

"My own grandchildren? My flesh and blood?"

"Unfortunately, yes."

"How did your men find this out, Tom?"

"They posed as homeless men and happened to see Michael and Vince one day. So they followed them to a restaurant where they were making plans for a party. They were sitting outside, so my men overheard their conversation," he says. "Michael and Vince are living the high life in Atlanta. They are renting a mansion and have a driver who also is their bodyguard. He's an older gentleman."

"Really? Continue."

"They saw Michael and Vince again at a restaurant called The Thyme. The restaurant was closed at the time, so they waited around until they came out. A few minutes after Michael and Vince went inside, another car pulled up, and two men got out. Our guys overheard the men say something about a drug deal with the Vecchios, but that's all they heard before the two men went inside."

"I am deeply saddened to hear this, Tom. I have done so much for Michael and Vince. This is how they repay me?"

"I am saddened too, but there's more."

"Go on."

"It took a while, but my men were able to get an invite, clean up and get into the party. The men who went into the restaurant after Michael and Vince are a part of a drug cartel, and there were prostitutes at the party. Here's what happened:

"Upon entering, they're asked for their invitation and proceed to join the festivities. There are about 100 men and scantily dressed women in attendance. They blend into the crowd, keeping their eyes out for the Vecchios and the men they'd seen meeting with them. About an hour into the party, they haven't seen them. They venture off in search of them in the mansion. Just as they turn a corner, they run into the bodyguard.

"'Will you look at this place? The Boss is not going to be pleased when he hears about this,' one of our men says as they enter the residence.

"'Gentlemen, can I help you?'

"'Uh, we were trying to find our way onto the terrace, but we must have made a wrong turn.'

"'Yes, you did. It's this way. Let me show you.'

"The men were escorted out onto the terrace, but as soon as the bodyguard leaves, they walked around the property to the area where they had been inside, hoping to find another way in. Just as they passed a window, someone came over and opened it. They could hear voices. One of the men put his mic on the windowsill. Here's the recording," Tom says, playing it for the group.

"*Michael, this deal needs to go down soon. No more stalling. When will you have the money?*"

"*My grandfather has eyes everywhere, so I have to be careful. I will have the rest of the money in a few days. These things take time. I'm trying to make a move here, and it can't be rushed. This deal is going down next week. When I receive the rest of the money, I'll call you to confirm a date.*"

"*Don't screw us, Michael. One more delay, and we're done.*"

"*Gentlemen, I promise, no more delays. I am putting my plans in place to make me the new Boss of the Vecchio family. No worries. Now go on out to the party and enjoy yourselves.*"

Tom stops the recording and says, "That happened two days ago."

"Michael is right. I do have eyes everywhere. I need to remind him and Vince who's Boss."

CHAPTER FIVE

In Atlanta, Detective Paul White is meeting with FBI agents Vincent Malone and Brad Guarino.

"Detective White, we thank you for meeting with us today. I hope it wasn't hard for you to get away."

"No, it wasn't. I used the guise of going to get the car washed."

"What have you found out?"

"The Vecchios had a party a few days ago, and the men from the cartel were in attendance. They are getting anxious because of the delays. Michael has been getting money in spurts so that he doesn't make his grandfather suspicious. He should be receiving the rest of the money tomorrow and setting a date for the deal."

"Wonderful. Let us know when the date has been set."

"Will do. I've been keeping an eye out for the prisoners who escaped, but I haven't seen them. There were two suspicious men at the party. I took their picture. Do you recognize either of them?"

"No, I don't. Do you, Brad?"

"No, but we will keep an eye out for them."

"We talked to the local police and have learned that someone is trying to set up the men who escaped from prison. One of their informants told them that someone is going to start killing cops and blame Carnell and James for the crimes. Now we have a cop killer on the loose."

"That's not good, not good at all. I will keep my eyes open. I better head out. Talk to you soon."

Agent Morris sits back in his chair after hanging up the phone. This case has taken a turn he had not expected. *What do Carnell Johnson and James Richardson have to do with the Vecchio family and the Manuel cartel?* He picks up the file he received on James Richardson and begins reading it again. *Who are you really, James Richardson?*

***

James and Carnell are in a car not far from The Thyme.

James says to Carnell, "This is where you and your boys were before they were murdered. You know this is where all of the crime bosses in Atlanta hang out?"

Carnell replies, "Yes. All we did was provide security and park cars. We were instructed to never get involved in a conversation with any of the members nor their guests. And we didn't."

James says, "I believe everything you're saying, but there may have been someone there who did not want to be seen— maybe someone from your past."

"I didn't see anyone I recognized."

"People are going in and out. We need to get closer. You may recognize someone."

The car moves closer to the restaurant. James is able to park in a place where it is undetected, but they have a full view.

"James, you see the man in the pin-striped suit? He was at the club the night my boys were murdered. The man walking beside him was there too."

James looks at the men and recognizes them as Edward Morgan and Justin Cooper, but he doesn't let on he knows them. He says, "I know some guys who work at the restaurant. I'll ask them about those men."

James and Carnell are being watched by Detective White. He writes down the license plate of their car. The windows are tinted, so he can't see who is inside. His instinct is telling him to watch the vehicle. The vehicle soon pulls off, and he decides to follow. He has some time to kill since he doesn't have to pick up Michael and Vince for another hour. Detective White follows the vehicle undetected to an abandoned building where he sees two men get out of the car and enter the building. He notices right away that one man is shorter than the other and lighter in complexion. He pulls up the photos of Carnell Johnson and James Richardson. Carnell is taller than James and darker. Coincidence? He's not sure, but since he now knows about this place, he will come back later.

***

"Hello."

"Grandfather, it's Michael."

"Michael, why are you in Atlanta?"

Michael lets out a gasp before he says, "Uh, uh ... Vince and I were invited to a party here in Atlanta, and we decided to stay a little longer since there was nothing pressing happening with the family."

"Michael, there is always something going on with the family. As my favorite grandson, I expect you to be the example for the others. That is why you have the position in this family that you have. You should always be available and know what is happening."

"I know, Grandfather, and I apologize for not being around."

"You have missed two meetings of the council, important meetings. And you were nowhere to be found. This is unacceptable, Michael. I have a lot to share with you, but I can't do that if you are in Atlanta doing who knows what. I am grooming you to take over, but another move like this, and I will have to rethink my decision."

"Grandfather, there's no need to rethink your decision. I appreciate everything that you have done for me. I will be returning to New York soon. Your birthday is coming up; I can't miss that."

Papa John sighs and says, "Michael, I have been the boss of this family for over 40 years, so I am no spring chicken. I know you're up to something. I expect your attendance the next time a council meeting is called. Remember, Michael, I have eyes everywhere. Don't cross me, Michael. Don't cross me. It will not turn out well."

"I understand, Grandfather," Michael says, and Papa John hangs up without saying goodbye.

"Sir," Detective White asks, "is everything okay?

Michael looks up and says, "Yes, yes it is."

***

Papa John is sitting in the library with Tom Palma when he hangs up from speaking with Michael.

"Don, did he say anything about inviting you to go to Sicily for your birthday?"

"No, he didn't. Should he have?"

"His plan is to get you out of the country and have you die in a plane crash and then he plans to take care of everyone on the council. That's what he told Sal."

"I know what has to be done now. It's time I announce my successor."

"Not Michael, I assume."

"No, not Michael. You are going to be my successor."

"Me?"

"Yes, you. You are my son and I trust you to take over. I know you will continue my legacy."

"Papa, are you sure?"

"Yes, I am. It's time I acknowledge you publicly. No more secrets," Papa John says. "I love my wife, but I also love your mother. Who knew one could fall in love with two women? She didn't want to get involved with me because I was married, but I persisted, and you and your sister are the results of our love."

"The family could turn on you once you make the announcement. I don't want that to happen to you, Papa John."

"I'm not worried about that. It's time to set things right and put Michael in his place."

***

When Detective White returns to the club to pick up Michael and Vince, they get in the car with another gentleman, Wayne Scott.

"Paul, please take us to the JW Marriott downtown. We have some business to discuss. We'll call you when we're ready to leave."

"Okay," Detective White replies and steers the car toward downtown.

During his time as driver/bodyguard for the Vecchios, Detective White had not seen them interact with Wayne Scott before, but he has seen him at The Thyme. He was able to take a picture of Scott before the men got in the car and sent it to Agent Morris.

After dropping them off, just as he is about to pull away from the hotel, he receives a text from Agent Morris asking if he could talk. He makes a call.

"Agent Morris, you have some information for me?"

"Yes. That picture of Wayne Scott you sent me is actually Roland Burris. Wayne Scott is one of his aliases. Although he has changed his look, we know he has a long rap sheet. He used to work for Carnell Johnson, and we believe he murdered Carnell's mother. We don't have anything concrete but believe he's been involved in a few murders. I just found out that he may be behind those attacks on Carnell in jail."

"Wow! I have seen him at The Thyme the last few times I was there. Today when he got in the car with the Vecchios, Michael said they had some business to discuss. He's staying at the JW Marriott downtown. I don't know what room because I didn't go up with them. I will receive a call when I need to return," Detective White says. "I have some business of my own to check out. I saw a couple of guys in a car outside the club recently, and I believe they are Carnell and James."

"They are back in Atlanta?"

"That's what I believe. I followed them to an abandoned building, and I am headed over there now to see if they are staying there."

"Detective, be careful. Let me know when you are going to pick up the Vecchios. I will have some men already at the hotel, and I will have them pick up Wayne Scott. If he's behind those attacks and Carnell and James are back in Atlanta, there could be a blood bath. We need to get him off the streets."

"Sure thing, and I'll let you know if these guys are Carnell and James."

A few minutes later, Detective White parks down the block from the abandoned building. As he approaches the building, he sees a light on in a window on the side of the building and goes to investigate. He sees Carnell and James and listens to their conversation through the cracked window.

Carnell asks, "James, were you able to find out who those guys were that we saw at The Thyme?"

"Yes, they're members of some kind of drug cartel trying to make a move on the East Coast. My boys said they have been in the area since you've been in jail and are ready to make a move up North."

"They don't take no mess. I remember when I first saw them. They got into an argument with someone they were meeting with, and the short dude up and popped the guy right between the eyes and walked away. I stayed my distance. I didn't know they were part of a cartel."

"That's what my boys told me. They said you don't want to cross them," James said. "You said they were there the night your boys were murdered?"

"Yes, they were having dinner."

"Do you think they had something to do with the murders?"

"Naw. We didn't have any interaction with them other than parking their car," Carnell said. "But one thing I do know is whoever killed my boys was close to me."

"So, you think it was someone from your crew?"

"It had to be. I just don't know who."

"Carnell, you must have pissed somebody off for them to turn on you like that."

"Pissing people off comes with the territory. I took care of my boys. We were tight."

"You weren't tight enough if one of them turned on you.

I believe whoever killed your boys put the hit out on you in jail."

"That makes sense. I need to find out who it is."

Detective White's phone buzzes in his pocket. He takes it out and sees a text from Michael saying they will be ready to leave in 15 minutes. He sends a reply saying he is on his way and heads back to his car. Once in his car, he calls Agent Morris.

"Agent Morris, today is a good day for the FBI. Those two guys are Carnell and James."

"That's great news. I'll notify my guys to move in when they see the Vecchios leave the hotel. They were able to get his room number. I'm not worried about Carnell and James tonight. I have to put some things in place before I can get them back in custody."

"Sounds like a plan. Carnell and James suspect that someone close to Carnell killed the three members of his gang and put the hit out on him."

"It's probably Roland. Soon after Carnell's mother was killed, Roland disappeared and created an alias for himself. I don't know what went down between them to make Roland kill Carnell's mother. Hopefully, we'll have the answer to that soon."

"I'm about to pull up to the hotel. I gotta hang up. Talk to you when I can."

As soon as the car comes to a stop, the Vecchios come through the door and enter the car. At the same time, the FBI agents go to the tenth floor, find Wayne Scott and arrest him.

CHAPTER SIX

A couple of days later, Michael received a call from Tom Palma informing him that he and Vince are to come to New York for a meeting of the council.

"I don't know if I can get there for the meeting. I have some business here in Atlanta to take care of that needs my attention."

"Michael, what kind of business is it?"

"I'd rather not say at this time. You'll just report back to Grandfather."

"He's the boss, Michael, and I'm loyal to him. I was directed to inform you of the meeting and to let you know that your presence is required. If you have other things to do, I will let the don know, and you will suffer the consequences. You've missed a couple of meetings already; you don't want to miss this one."

"Yes, I know. It's just that things are coming ... never mind. Did Grandfather say what this meeting is about?"

"He said something about a big announcement. You better make sure you're here to hear it in person, Michael."

"I'll see what I can do."

"Is that what you want me to tell your grandfather, you 'will see what you can do'?"

Michael sighs and says, "Tell him I'll be there."

"Wonderful," Tom says and hangs up.

Michael turns to Vince and says, "Grandfather has called a meeting the same day our deal is to go down."

"I can stay and handle the deal."

"He wants both of us to attend the meeting. The cartel won't like this."

"Don't let them know. Just show up late. We can do both in one day."

"They'll be pissed when they can't reach me."

"The Manuel cartel are going to be pissed if you call them about another delay. There's no way around it. We'll go to the meeting, get back here as soon as we can and deal with it then."

"Okay."

***

Roland Burris has been interrogated by the FBI agents for the last couple of days and reveals that Edward Morgan and Justin Cooper hired him to kill Carnell Johnson because Carnell could identify Michael. It was ironic because Roland had a secret. Roland had created an alias for himself, Wayne Scott, and was ready to come back to Atlanta to make a move on Carnell's territory. In his heart, he had gotten the ultimate payback already, since he had murdered Carnell's mother in retaliation. As far as he was concerned, they were even. But Edward and Justin had figured out that he had murdered Carnell's mother and threatened to reveal the secret. At this point, it was kill or be killed.

He and Carnell fell out because Roland had given drugs to Carnell's girlfriend at the time without her knowledge and raped her. Carnell had wanted revenge and went looking for Roland. When he found him, Carnell aimed his gun and fired. He shot Roland and Roland's mother, who had been standing behind him. When the bullet exited Roland, it hit his mother. Carnell didn't know the bullet had also struck her. In retaliation, Roland tracked down and shot Carnell's mother, but his shot was deadly. Not wanting the information to get out, he came up with a plan to make it look like Carnell had killed his own men, then he disappeared. He also ordered the hits on Carnell in prison. In exchange for a shorter sentence, he told the agents about the deal between Edward, Justin and the Vecchios and that it would be going down soon.

***

Agent Morris sets up the plan to bring in Carnell and James so they can be put into protective custody. His agents arrive at the abandoned building, but the escapees are not there. However, it's not long before they arrive. The agents notice that the local police have also arrived. Agent Malone heads over to one of the cars and identifies himself. The officer tells him they received a tip that the escapees were hiding in this building. Agent Malone tells him that is the reason the FBI are there and that they would be taking charge. After a brief discussion, everyone gets in place. The agents and police move in on Carnell and James. As they are leading them out of the building, James suddenly falls down. They realize he has been shot but don't know what direction the bullet came from. Soon, a few police are also shot before everyone runs for cover. One of the agents sees a shadow across the street and fires his gun, but the person gets away.

James is rushed to the hospital, and Carnell is driven to a safe house outside Atlanta.

***

Michael and Vince arrive in New York a day before the council meeting. Two hours before they were scheduled to go to the meeting, Michael was trying to reach Vince but couldn't. Michael didn't want to upset his grandfather by not showing up, so he got into the car that was sent for him. He arrives at a warehouse where his grandfather sometimes holds council meetings. When he enters the building, he is guided to a back room, making the hairs on the back of his neck stand up. Where he is being led is not the meeting room. As the door opens, he sees his grandfather, Papa John Vecchio, standing over his cousin Vince, who is lying in a pool of blood.

"Michael, I'm so glad you could grace us with your presence."

"Grandfather."

"Vince told us about the deal you have with the Manuel cartel. He was not forthcoming with the information at first, so we had to beat it out of him."

Michael looks over at Vince, wondering how his grandfather is going to kill him.

"What have I done to you to make you want to go off on your own?"

"Nothing, Grandfather."

"Nothing?? It has to be something in order for you to turn your back on your family. I have taken good care of you and Vince. Have I not?"

"Yes, Grandfather."

"This is how you repay me? Our family does not deal in

drugs or prostitution, Michael. But you wanted to take the family in a different direction and make more money. Money is the root of all evil. Michael, what happens to people who turn their backs on their family?"

"They are taken care of."

"Yes, they disappear. I had plans for you Michael, big plans. I will be 75 soon and am planning to retire to enjoy the rest of my life. I have already announced that Tom will take over as Boss. He's your uncle and has been loyal to me since the day I brought him into the family."

"My uncle?"

"Yes, from an affair I had many years ago. You were to become his right-hand man, Michael, but you messed it up."

"An affair? You cheated on Grandmother and brought the child into the family?"

"Now is not the time for you get all high and mighty, Michael. When your grandmother found out, she didn't leave me, she stayed. And I love her for that. I can't say the same for you. It's going to break her heart when she finds out about what I had to do."

The Boss walks over to Michael, kisses him and says, "I love you, Michael. There is nothing more important than family." With a tear in his eye, he turns and walks away. He and Tom exit the room as the lieutenants walk over to Michael to do what needs to be done. Papa John is relieved to know his family will continue the tradition his grandfather started.

CHAPTER SEVEN

Agent Morris, Detective White and Agent Woody are in a meeting when Agent Morris says, "Detective White, thank you for your assistance. You were very helpful."

"I enjoyed it. I am glad most of the players are in custody. Once I dropped the Vecchios off at the airport, I never heard from them again. Have you found them?"

"No, we haven't. I don't think we will either. The Mafia takes care of their own. I'm sure his grandfather found out what he was doing and took care of things. But we have Roland Burris, Edward Morgan and Justin Cooper in custody. Roland sung like a bird, and he's looking at a lot of time in prison for several murders. Morgan and Cooper are looking at a long time behind bars as well."

"And what about James Richardson?"

"James is actually an FBI agent. He and Carnell were friends when they were young."

Detective White says, "I never would have guessed."

"My cousin was put in charge as warden of the prison and when he told me about the hits on Carnell's life, I sent James in to see what was going on inside and try to find out who was behind those hits."

"This got deep, quickly," Detective White says. "So, their escape was planned?"

"An escape was planned, but not that soon. James kind of went rogue on me for a while. Paul, I think I grew a few more hairs turn gray dealing with my cousin and James."

Paul and David laugh.

David says, "Randall, you deserve a vacation after all of this."

"I know, and I plan on taking one real soon."

"Is Carnell still at the safe house?"

"Yes, he is until all of the trials have been completed. He is going to be a witness in all three trials."

"Well, I hope he can turn his life around," Paul says.

"I have talked to him, and he says once this is all over, he is going to move to a small town in Arkansas named Helena. He's tired of his life."

"Helena!? That's where I'm from."

"He says his sister is married to a police officer there, Michael Hamilton."

"Are you kidding me? He helped me with a case in Helena. It's a small world."

"It sure is, Detective. It sure is."

ABOUT THE AUTHOR

Otis Jones is a retired United States Postal Worker who started to write mysteries late in life, finding extra time in his 60s, to be creative. Born in Helena, Arkansas, the author brings imagination and old-fashioned crime solving to his stories, often named in honor of old friends from the past.

www.ingramcontent.com/pod-product-compliance
Lightning Source LLC
Chambersburg PA
CBHW020616120726
47905CB00003B/821